LEARNING TO DRIVE

. . .

LEARNING TO DRIVE

. . .

William Norwich

THE ATLANTIC MONTHLY PRESS
NEW YORK

The author wishes to acknowledge Ed Victor Ltd., Morgan Entrekin, Colin Dickerman, and the generosity of his employers Anna Wintour and Arthur L. Carter.

Published simultaneously in Canada
Printed in the United States of America
FIRST EDITION

Library of Congress Cataloging-in-Publication Data

Norwich, William D.
Learning to drive / William Norwich.
p.   cm.
ISBN 0-87113-631-7
I. Title.
PS3564.0778L43 1996
813'.54–dc20   95-53099

DESIGN BY LAURA HAMMOND HOUGH

Atlantic Monthly Press
841 Broadway
New York, NY 10003

10 9 8 7 6 5 4 3 2 1

TO A CERTAIN CIRCLE OF FRIENDS

As I sd to my
friend, because I am
always talking, —John, I

sd, which was not his
name, the darkness sur-
rounds us, what

can we do against
it, or else, shall we &
why not, buy a goddamn big car,

drive, he sd, for
christ's sake, look
out where yr going.
                    —ROBERT CREELEY,
                        "I Know a Man"

ONE

...

Learn to drive, learn to drive, learn to drive . . . it wasn't for some sudden love of cars that it was due time, at age thirty-seven, that I learned to drive.

"Did I ever mention that my father sold Pontiacs? That this obsession with learning to drive, or not learning to drive as the case may be, goes way back?" I asked Ines Spring.

Ines sighed. She was my finely tuned employer, the editor in chief of the fashion magazine *View*, and a friend, too, I liked to think. We were seated together at a charity party in New York several so-called social seasons ago; the beneficiary of this evening's efforts was one of the local ballet companies. I also wrote a daily around-the-town column for the *Tribune*; I was there to cover the do for the tabloid. It was close to midnight, it had been a long evening—cocktails first, the performance of several new dances including an homage to shifting sexual identities that involved costumes of drag and some thirty dancers leaping to the scratched sounds of progressive, computerized disco, and then the dinner. The salad plates were just cleared by a fleet of handsome waiters who, in their black jackets and polished poses, were, as was customary in New York in the late 1980s, more attractive than the majority of the guests. The promise of things in cream and veal awaited us; a thousand black-tied people whirled and twirled on the dance floor—"La Bamba," a punishingly bouncy south-of-the-border tune, had gotten the assembly of Manhattan's most noted movers and shakers to the dance floor. The pay-to-attend charity ball replaced disco in this decade; the ladies' dresses were as bold as strobes—they shined expense.

Ines and I hardly overflowed with pep, let alone mirth. We protected each other from having to dance. We could not quite see the guests at the other side of the table, so tall were the jungled centerpieces.

"Did I ever mention that? That my father was blue-eyed and gray-haired and had a future like the moon's?"

"What are you talking about, Julian—your father had a future like the moon's?" Ines asked, fidgeting impatiently with the gold clasp on her evening bag.

"When you cannot see the sky, you are promised the moon," I tried to explain.

"Darling, why don't you have a drink," she said and almost cried at the sight of a fashion designer we knew dancing with a woman in a $25,000 couture, leather bondage dress. "Tie a Yellow Ribbon" around the old oak tree was the song the band played now; it always seemed to follow "La Bamba" on society nights.

"Anyway, my shrink is really after me to learn to drive. He says that if I do, I can drive to where my parents are buried and put my past to rest," I said, thinking of a session with my worthy doctor that afternoon.

"I suppose," Ines responded, her British accent an economy of pear-shaped tones.

"I haven't been to the cemetery since my mother was buried there nearly twenty years ago," I continued.

"And where is it?" Ines asked.

"In southeastern Connecticut," I explained. "Near Goldenrod, where I was born and raised, nearly a three-hour drive from here."

"Why don't you just hire a car and driver?" Ines suggested.

"The shrink thinks that it would be too much of an eighties thing to do, too catered. The whole point of the exercise, he says, is for me to learn to drive and drive there myself," I said. "It's as much a metaphor as it is practical."

"I see that, Julian." Ines smiled and patted me on the arm.

"Of course," I said.

The waiters sailed toward us with their plates of veal. The guests followed the fleet and returned to their seats at the dressed tables. Photographers dodged the waiters to take pictures of the guests. "My husband has been after me to learn to drive, too," Ines said. "We might as well; you and I have been talking about this for a while. Make the arrangements tomorrow with whatever is the best driving school; let's get this done before I go to the couture in July."

"How old were you exactly when your parents died?" asked the socialite with bumblebee-yellow hair seated at my other side. I hadn't realized she was listening to our conversation.

Ines studied the veal on her plate with the caterer's fork. I looked into the emeralds squeezed between the diamonds on the socialite's new necklace. "Oh, let's not go there tonight," I suggested with all the charm I could muster.

"Why ruin the party?"

TWO

...

We heard a car crash once.

When I was growing up in Goldenrod, we heard a car crash. It was the summer of 1962; I think a Tuesday night. We received a delivery that afternoon from the biggest department store in Hartford, where we shopped – almost three hours away from the city, Goldenrod was not a suburb of New York, at least not yet – and the delivery was a black cashmere winter coat with a mink collar for my mother, Leah, whom my father loved, although he slept in their bed with me and my mother slept in another room.

My father and I were asleep, my mother was asleep in another room, and my grandparents, my father's parents, my zayde and my bubbie, who dispensed sour candies and kisses with her sharp, crusty lips, were asleep in their apartment upstairs. We lived in a Victorian house with a porch built all around it and mezuzahs blessing the doorway to each room. On the back lawn was a sundial and all my father's roses.

I did not recognize the sound of cars crashing. My father put on his robe, and I followed him to the front porch, where we saw two cars rolled practically into one.

To witness, the neighbors' silhouettes flooded the shadows on their porches. My mother opened the front screen door and stood there for a minute before she joined us on the porch. There wasn't an evening wind; there were waves of neighborhood chatter instead of breeze. My mother ran a hand through her auburn-red hair; it fanned the nape of her neck like a veil. She closed her pink robe across her white silk negligee and studied my father with some surprise, as if she had forgotten him in her sleep.

"Who are they?" she asked.

My father walked to the sidewalk, near to the cars.

"They're from out of town," he said when he returned to the porch. The street filled with police cars and ambulances.

From their porches, the neighbors withdrew, the men in pajama bottoms and day-old T-shirts, the women in cotton wrappers, unlike my mother. My grandmother, long, white hair down from its bun for sleeping, opened the screen door and watched the accident. "Who are they?" she asked in Yiddish.

My father answered he did not know.

"Jewish?" my grandfather wondered over my grandmother's shoulder.

"No, Pa, I shouldn't think so," my father answered.

My grandfather shrugged and took my grandmother back to bed. My mother lighted a Pall Mall and studied my father. Her silk robe fell open; she flicked the cigarette ashes into her hand and went inside before the cigarette was out. I took my father's hand and walked along the porch to the back yard of the house. I wasn't wearing slippers, and I remember the grass was cold and wet like seaweed at low tide. Barefoot, I sunk into the lawn. The blades of grass seemed almost hip-length.

"Have you ever seen my roses sleep, Jules?"

"No, sir."

He put his hand behind my neck. My nose went toward a tight cluster of my father's pink roses closed like fists against the windless night.

We walked back to the front of the house to look. The ambulances left the accident without sounding their sirens; years later I learned this meant the people were dead. I followed my father into our house. He locked the door, which he didn't always, and we went to bed. I apologized for the wet blades of grass on my feet; my father told me to sleep. He rolled me in his arms. His chest hairs were like thorns.

THREE

...

And, so, the very next morning after the charity ball I telephoned McCaulay's Driving School, located just a few blocks from my apartment on Manhattan's Upper East Side.

McCaulay's advertised on matchbooks and in subways; one knew of people, even myopic, middle-aged people, who went to McCaulay's and somehow learned to drive. Quite a few adults in New York do not have licenses; I considered this tremendous consolation. "No need for embarrassment that you cannot drive," offered the Jamaican-accented woman who answered the phone when I called the driving school.

"It's just that when I was a teenager the circumstances weren't quite right for me to learn to drive, and then, well, I moved to Manhattan, and you really don't need to drive here so, well . . . "

"It's okay, we'll be happy to teach you," she said kindly.

"And I really don't consider myself a good candidate for driving; I can't imagine I will be any good at it. I can't see terribly well, although I do wear corrective contact lenses. And I think I'm much too, well, spacey, distracted, I mean, to be allowed on a highway for more than a few minutes. I mean, I'll never be able to play the radio and drive at the same time if I am to maintain my focus on the road . . . "

"It's okay, sir, it's okay," the woman consoled me. "Everybody gets a license when they enroll at McCaulay's," she promised. She described the details and the time required of us: five hours of classroom and then off to meet the masses at the Motor Vehicle Department for the written and eye exams – extensive proof of one's identity was necessary, she explained – and then, after passing those tests and receiving one's learner's permit would come the business of actually going out on the New York City roads and highways with an instructor who could teach even the dizziest of customers how to drive. The lady who answered the phone at McCaulay's promised me.

All of this I conveyed to Ines between racks of red satin Oscar de la Renta ballgowns and pink wool Chanel suits that had been delivered into her window-lined office for inspection that morning by a variety of fashion editors. The accessories editor, who also did not drive, got up to leave Ines's office as soon as I entered with my opening salvo: "Ines, we're going to learn to drive! They'll have us at McCaulay's."

The accessories editor, holding a large glazed-straw tray filled with the latest Cartier and Bulgari watches, shuddered. "The next thing you know it will be driving gloves and Porsche watches in the magazine," she warned us disapprovingly.

We selected a period of days before the Memorial Day holiday that suited Ines's schedule. I called the lady at McCaulay's and booked our lessons. I was optimistic; progress was to be made. At lunchtime, when everyone made off to the Royalton or the Four Seasons for the midday meal, I switched on my computer and wrote my newspaper column for the next day. It was easy enough; I described last night's benefit: the chateau-sized dresses, the dance, who was there. It wasn't difficult for anyone who chronicled social New York in the 1980s; all one had to do was write what they – the constant characters – spent and what they said about what they spent and one had a column. In New York's boom-boom 1980s, everything was big! The bigger, the better. Status in New York was no longer just about what you did or who you knew; it was measured by how much space (physical space, column space) you took up.

Silly me. When I took the job of a columnist in 1985, I thought it was about writing and was delighted. A job in which one got to entertain a readership while honing one's craft seemed too good to imagine. But as time went on, I learned the column wasn't about writing – no one cared about the writing – it was about tabulating names. "Ah, yes, the keeper of the lists," said a well-known artist of a certain age when we met, by chance, at a gallery early on in my column-writing career.

Most people approved of the columns that mentioned the names of people they liked – and they especially liked it when they were themselves mentioned. They disliked those columns that mentioned those they disdained. Nonetheless, writing the column provided a hectic pace: five days a week at about nine hundred words each and no sick days (who would write the column?). A doyenne of the business, Mary Smythe, who got me my first column by persuading her bosses at the *Tribune* to take me on, has likened the craft to riding a tiger; you dare not get off lest it eat you.

So I became one of the more popular bulletin boards around – a skin upon which people posted their most vainglorious notices – lost in the hope, as the expression goes, that I might find myself later when I had the time. But I should say a few things about myself before I get too involved. I needed the money when I took the job. I have been broke even more times than I have been a virgin, meaning the long periods one knows without any currency of affection. My name is Julian Orr. I was born thirty-seven years ago in summertime. My father was born in Russia in 1895. He came to America in 1900; he was the eldest of five sons and sold tires and Pontiacs so his siblings could attend college and find themselves decent professions. My mother was born in Goldenrod in 1914; her parents were born there, too, of Scottish-Jewish ancestors who settled in Connecticut after the Civil War. My father died when I was nine, my mother when I was seventeen; I was their only child. I got by; I educated myself by accruing some big debts. My affliction was I wanted to become a writer. Not very practical. I read once that when Joan Didion was starting out, she lived off the food she could charge in gourmet shops at department stores. I thought if I charged escargot like she had at Bloomingdale's I'd be on my way toward a great literary tradition. Instead, my charge cards were taken away. I knocked around; I managed to get a B.A. from a college in western Massachusetts on the layaway plan. My student loans had loans. I moved to New York City, where most everyone I met who wanted to become a writer had a trust fund or helpful kin; I held a series of odd jobs—waiter, cleaner, postcard seller at Fiorucci—and went home to a one-room studio my friends thought was colorful.

Fatigued by my half-baked days, I went to bed early except for a brief spurt of energy during the Studio 54 disco days that left me exhausted, physically and financially, when the dancing feast moved to places like the Mudd Club and Area.

A friend who wanted to become a writer was accepted at a graduate writing program in the city, and she suggested I apply as well. I was accepted on the basis of a portfolio of pathetic poems about loneliness and a short story I'd actually published in a punk rock magazine about a cat who became a socialite. I didn't know how to pay for graduate school – $10,000 a year for tuition, and that didn't even include a cup of afternoon tea – and was excited when I landed a job as a script writer for a television soap opera. That and student loans, and I could cuddle up in the paternal lap of higher education. Graduate school commenced: with occasional exceptions a toothful, sharklike pool of forty students about whom all I could wonder is, How are they affording this? I remember one southern professor warning us not to write about feet: "Why bring your reader's eye down to the ground when you should lift them up with your prose?" she asked, grinding her dragged-out cigarette into the linoleum floor of our academia. Ten days into graduate school I was fired from the soap opera. Once again I was broke and in debt. I read Proust, began a phase in which I wrote only ghost stories, got a job washing dishes in an espresso bar, and told myself someday it would all work out.

Ah, yes: the hot-air balloons of youth.

To add that fall to my income as a dishwasher, an acquaintance recommended me for a job ghost writing for the ghost writer of a gossip column. It was the early 1980s. The literature of the social vanities, the work of E. F. Benson and Nancy Mitford, for instance, had always appealed to me: sophisticated people saying smart things and meaning not what they said, the penalties of enforced frivolity. My success, if you will, ghost writing for the ghost writer caught the attention of Mary Smythe; she befriended me and helped me find more work. If you could meet a deadline, you could get assignments. You were needed on the magazines and newspapers that devoted increasing space to chronicling the buffets and bouquets of all the new money people who towered over the cityscape. When the around-the-town column on the *Tribune* became available, Mary Smythe convinced them to give me the job. (I think she was tired of my borrowing money from her.)

I went from being basically unemployed to being over-employed in a matter of days; I felt shot out of a cannon. I had never understood what one is supposed to do with oneself at cocktail parties and disliked them; now it was my job to attend sometimes four a night. On Saturdays, the one day of the week I didn't have to work, a sorrowfulness would sweep over me until I went to bed early, often sedated, by nine at night. It never occurred to me that I had lost my way; I was just paying the rent. It was like sportswriting: I covered teams and games and re-ported on the players' progress. I never for a second thought I was at home anyplace other than the stands, an observer. I did not want to be a player; I waited and hoped to be saved and brought, somehow, somewhere else, into the rink of some kind of familial life. Then I would become a real writer. Meanwhile, I dressed myself in uniforms — one blue, one black Armani suit — and thought I could deduct the expense of my dinner jackets from my taxes. What else did one such as myself wear to work? Despite my role as promoter of an elite, I was a child of the sixties, whose pea brain, even in the middle of a charity ball, might suddenly chime with Laura Nyro lyrics about the chambered walls of heartache.

Sometimes the newspaper I wrote for would go on strike or nearly out of business; the employees nervously awaited new buyers. There were plenty of what I called lame-duck days when the phone wouldn't ring. I took solace in the humbling experi-ence: only everyone else — my new best friends — thought I was my job. I didn't know who I was, but I wasn't the job, the smiling head without a body pictured over the daily column. Seeking what I hoped might be more creative employment, I was eager to join my acquaintance Ines Spring when she came from England to edit *View*. I was set up with an office at the magazine—I had been working from home, filing copy to the newspaper through a mysterious, to me, fax-modem—and was given some money and some feature writing to do. I had happened upon this soapbox; I'd been writing about how, in the 1980s, it was all about money, but come the 1990s, the message, socially speaking, would be the Mix. This Mix business, although short-lived, captured a few imaginations and had its parallels in the world of fashion: the wearing of, say, a couture Lacroix jacket with an old pair of jeans. Democrats were getting themselves elected for the moment rather than Republicans, and "the Mix" became the advertising slogan for one of the local radio stations: light music, hard rock, popular love songs—about as good as it gets.

The Monday evening before the Memorial Day holiday, Ines and I matriculated at McCaulay's Driving School in the East Eighties in Manhattan. The school was located in the basement of an apartment house on one of those New York City streets that never sees sunlight; the color is oil-gray, the buildings seem parentless. Ines wore a white suit with crossed black lines that looked like abstract road maps; her children, a young boy and little girl, bought her a notebook to take with her to school. There were about a dozen of us, an aromatic mix of teenagers and foreign-born driving students. Ines never removed her dark, prescription glasses even when the room was darkened for the presentation of two hours' worth of films about car crashes and drunk driving.

We returned to McCaulay's the next night and watched more films—dummies flying through windshields was a recurring motif—and spent hours listening to our earnest classroom instructor tell us how to prepare the various forms of identification we would need to present at the Motor Vehicle office. We could go as a group in a McCaulay's van to the MV that Friday morning; Ines whispered we would go, instead, in her chauffeur-driven car.

And that is what we did: 7:30 on Friday morning, sunny weather, Ines's car fetched me, and we went downtown to the Department of Motor Vehicles, a yellowing space congested with closed windows and a thousand or so New Yorkers gone prickly in heated lines. I wore a blue suit; Ines wore black trousers and a black Chanel sweater that buttoned in the back with some fifty tiny gold logo medallions from the French fashion house. We were standing in line for our eye exams when the young woman behind me reached past and started fastening buttons Ines had missed in her morning's haste.

Ines, who was reading the editorial page of the *Times*, did not flinch. "Oh, thank you," she said to the woman.

"Go on, girl; you're looking good now—good as last week when I saw you on *Good Morning America*." She gave Ines her business card; she worked in a bank. The next day Ines sent the Chanel sweater around with a year's subscription to *View*. Ines did things like that, especially back then.

Ines passed the eye exam without removing her sunglasses; she admitted to the examiner that she was practically blind without them. I passed with my hands shaking and my contact lenses dry as toast. I hadn't slept well the night before; I'd begun having these dreams about driving: that night I had dreamt that I was on the turnpike headed home, but I kept shrinking behind the wheel until I could not see over the dashboard.

The written test was too logical; I almost failed. Question number three: If you are entering the highway, do you a) stop on the entrance ramp; b) flow into the traffic; c) honk your horn until the lane is yours? "What's the answer?" I whispered to Ines.

"The answer is b," she responded.

The exam monitor separated us. "No talking please," she said.

It seemed an eternity while our exams were graded. Then, eureka, we passed. Ines and I received learner's permits valid for one year, during which time we would learn to drive and, hopefully, pass our road exams and get licenses once and for all.

"I feel so free, I feel so free—isn't it weird, but I do!" I exclaimed in the limousine to the office.

"Going to hit the road, Julian?" Ines asked.

"Going to hit the road, Ines," I said.

Our luck in learning to drive divided there, however. Ines, supremely organized, immediately arranged for a McCaulay's driving teacher to tutor her several mornings during the coming weeks. They would drive through the quiet streets of post-dawn SoHo, where Ines lived; she caught on to the driving thing quite naturally. One morning she even drove her two children to school in the McCaulay's car and arrived cool as good news at the office by a quarter to nine. She passed her road test and got her license a few days before the Fourth of July holiday. That weekend in the country, she drove once, to get the Sunday newspaper and, thinking she was still in England, drove on the left side of the road. She hasn't driven since, but the point is, she got her license.

I, on the other hand, was plagued by these awful driving dreams; I'd wake up in a sweat just in time to get into the McCaulay's car with any one of several instructors, all of whom thought I was a total loser: a thirty-seven-year-old white male who didn't know how to drive? We would drive away from my street in the East Seventies and head toward Gracie Mansion uptown. When we'd start, it was still early enough in the morning—7 A.M.—so there wasn't much traffic, but minute by minute the streets filled with taxis and cars and trucks, and I'd panic. The instructor would sip his coffee and swallow his donut. I might brake for no obvious reason other than my fear; I apologized profusely to the teacher.

We discussed this in therapy, of course. Spring became summer, then fall turned into winter, and eventually I stopped dreaming I was shrinking behind the wheel of a car. When for several nights in a row I dreamed I could see over the steering wheel, I arranged for another series of driving lessons from McCaulay's; eventually an instructor thought I might pass an actual exam, and an appointment was made. I should mention that it is easier to get orchestra seats for the latest Broadway show with frontal nudity than it is to secure an appointment for a road test. Due to demand, these appointments take weeks to get; mine was scheduled for a morning in early May, three weeks before my learner's permit expired, and, please no, I would have to begin the process of learning to drive again if I failed. Getting a driver's license had become my obsession. On the appointed morning the telephone rang, and it was the head of McCaulay's calling to apologize: the instructor meant to drive me to the Motor Vehicle Department in Yonkers was sick.

"Impossible!" I yelled into the phone.

"We'll reschedule," the McCaulay's man said.

"Don't you see that is impossible? It took three weeks to get this appointment; in three more weeks my learner's permit will have expired. You'll have to do something; pull strings. I'll pull strings; I've got to get there!"

I think seasons of deadlines had made me more hysterical than I would like to admit. I really believed if you passed beyond the time for which you had been contracted, you were dead; in the newspaper business missing a deadline certainly made you unpopular. So I found someone who knew someone who knew someone else who could arrange for me to take my road test at the Motor Vehicle office in Brooklyn, not Yonkers, where the Mc-Caulay's people preferred to go. I made my appointment for a morning two weeks later, and the head of McCaulay's said, although they preferred Yonkers, he would arrange for one of his instructors to take me.

"Don't worry; it'll all work out," the shrink said when I told him the story.

"Hasn't it been a year? Maybe it's an omen," Ines remarked.

What came next was unpredictable. When I tell the story, I try to tell it lightly. "Oh, yes, I unraveled in broad daylight on the Belt Parkway," I might say.

The newspaper accounts tell a much different story.

FOUR

. . .

Sometimes, on summer days be-
fore he died, my father would take me motoring.

"Do you like trains?" he asked the morning after the cars
crashed.

"Yes, sir," I answered.

We were always a quiet house. In winter we were covered
with snow as high as a child; in summer the lawn went emerald
green and the sunlight on the leaves of the trees was hyp-
notic. Our life was a long lull maintained by generally kindly
people who never got themselves out of place. My father cared
for his roses; my mother dressed and smoked and talked on
the telephone.

"Then I've got a treat for you today," my father said.

We were on the back lawn near the flowers. My mother
opened the screen door and walked toward us. She wore a black
hat and white gloves and her blue linen dress; she waved goodbye
and drove off in the gray and white Pontiac.

"Are we going to the garage?" I asked as my father took me
inside and helped dress me in white shorts and a striped polo
shirt. I was eight years old. My mother didn't like my going to the

garage, in case I got hurt, she said. It was okay if I stayed in the showroom, among the new cars for sale, but in the garage with the mechanics something might happen.

"No," my father replied. "Let's go see the trains. You've never seen a real one, have you?"

Not only does everything seem bigger when you are a child, but colors are more vivid, and all motion, because you are not yet preoccupied with time, seems more fluid. You still are on forever terms with the world, especially an only child. No sibling gets there first; no one colors the light or changes the sounds before you do. We drove in a green Pontiac from our street in town to the outskirts; although it was only a twenty-minute ride to the next town, it felt like several countries away separated by fields, one or two mansions, an outdoor egg market, and a private hospital with a long driveway lined with elm trees and stone walls. I knew that was where the people with polio were kept inside iron lungs you saw pictures of in the newspapers my father left on the porch. You could go swimming that summer and wake up and might never walk again.

We drove. My father wore a blue seersucker suit and a brown straw hat with a red feather in its black band. At New London, the road became manicured and curved. On the left were soldiers doing their drills on the lawn of the Coast Guard Academy. On the right, pitched on a hill, was a woman's college. We drove deeper into the village and parked the Pontiac near a stucco building on Long Island Sound. The train station, my father explained.

There were the sights of a shipyard and a ferry in the sound; from the east came my first train. It made noise worse than the cars that crashed the night before, worse than a thunderstorm, and it came too fast, like it could steal you from the ground. What was wrong with me—why did I cry? I cried until I saw that the strangers who got off the train were mostly met by other strangers who were so glad to see them. An engineer in the last train waved to me; my father, who had pulled some strings to arrange this greeting, told me to wave back.

I did. We waved and waved, and people smiled; I sensed my father's pleasure in having produced something today even more spectacular than last night's car crash. "New York is where the trains go, Jules," he said. "Your mother and I have been there." It was so quiet when the train left, I felt it had left me. We got back into the Pontiac, which smelled new, crisp, and of leatherette; we drove to my uncle Daniel's house not far from the station. Uncle Daniel's was a proud house that was big and white with too many rooms for children to be left alone when they played; I'd been there before. There was the briny smell of the sound and the constant sound of the water on the sand. My cousin Alan was there, round-faced and pudgy but a superior student, or so I'd been told; we were like two foreigners docked on the same island by our relations. My father had brought for me a change of clothes; I entered a bathing cottage separate from the main house—there were five cabins for changing, each one with pegs from which stray bathing suits hung like weak handkerchiefs—and emerged in a pair of new trunks decorated with a seahorse print.

Alan and I swam, although I didn't really know how. The crests of the waves rolled over us like cold shaken milk. "Your father is old," Alan said as I buried my hands in the sand and let the water wash over my back. I knew that my father was old by most standards; everyone got around to telling me sooner or later, as if I was incapable of knowing this myself. What did people mean when they told me he was old? That he loved me less, or that he would leave us that much sooner?

"So, I told him, Saul, 'Go screw yourself, Senator, I don't care who you are," Uncle Daniel said. My father, the trousers of his seersucker suit rolled to his knees, pulled me from the water when I began tumbling into the sea. I coughed foam against his dress shirt; he listened to his brother's story. One of Uncle Daniel's immediate neighbors was a United States senator, the only Jewish senator at that time. As my uncle told it, our senator had walked absentmindedly this morning on my uncle's new sidewalk before the cement had hardened; Uncle Daniel had told him off and was proud to have done so.

My father's hand led me from the shore; wasn't I drowning? My uncle wore a gray business suit. He was a big executive for a utilities company, and from his porch you could see the senator and his family on their porch, which was measurably bigger. An American flag was unfurled; there were laughing ladies in wide-brimmed hats and pastel dresses.

Cousin Alan and I changed from our bathing suits in the cabana. "My mother says we're cousins, but we are once re-moved," Alan said, pleased by his mother's permission to disas-sociate. Like two white candles without flames, we stood naked in the cabana looking at each other. "We're going to Israel," Alan said. "Next month, to visit a kibbutz." His two brown eyes, dull as stones, shined suddenly with daring.

It was sunless inside the cabana; the smell was of damp bathing suits and spilt lotions. Alan stood, shifting his consider-able weight from bare foot to bare foot; he fondled himself between his legs—against the soft dough of his thighs he could have been putting a worm on a fishhook. "And you don't have any brothers or sisters—that's weird," Alan said.

"But I will someday."

"Will not," Alan insisted.

The door to the cabana opened with a bang; Alan jumped into his shorts.

"Aren't you boys dressed yet?" Uncle Daniel called.

"Be right there, Grandpa," Alan answered.

Uncle Daniel walked us to the Pontiac. My father started the engine; my uncle closed the car door behind me and stuck his head in the window. "I owe you a toy," he told me, his breath smelling of luncheon pickles and tea, "for coming to see me and being such a good boy. And don't lose any sleep over that accident last night, Julian, your father told me all about it. When it's your time to go, it's your time to go."

"Daniel, really, he's just a little boy," my father told his brother.

We drove home. "Why can't I have a brother or sister?" I asked my father.

"Are you that lonely, Jules?" my father wondered.

From his words, suddenly, the concept of loneliness was drawn for the first time, like a blueprint for a new pool on the lawn.

My father was a cautious driver. Slowly we surfed the hills and curves of the crystalline Connecticut exurbia. I watched him drive; I appointed myself his copilot. With his square jaw and sapphire blue eyes and melancholy smile, I thought my father was terrifically handsome; I never find even the vaguest map of his lost face in mine.

"Cousin Alan is going to Israel," I said after some silence.

"I know. How about that?"

I shrugged.

"Would you like to go to Israel?" my father asked.

"Why?"

"Well, why not? It is the homeland of all Jewish people," he said.

There were not many Jewish people in Goldenrod, except for my relations and a few other families; I had discovered our minority almost the first day of public school a few years before. The realization came with my introduction to daily school prayer and, later, Christmas parties; I was partial to both. One never sensed that, as a Jew in Goldenrod, one was unwelcome, but there were unspoken expectations, suspicions that such immediate European ancestries meant we were perhaps a bit, well, different: we were never the first people asked to play in Goldenrod's Little League and we rarely barbecued.

"New dress?" my father asked my mother when we returned home.

My mother was sitting on the back porch, reading a novel.

"Actually, yes," she answered, standing up to model her confection of black and white polka dots cinched tight at her waist. She lighted a Pall Mall and exhaled slowly. She poured my father a highball from a crystal canteen on the serving wagon nearby; my mother cupped the ice long enough in her hand that the cubes bled spring water over her diamond ring. I would remember this at the Sotheby's auction years later when I tried to sell the ring to pay for graduate school (but the bids came in under the reserve, less than one year's tuition). My mother dropped the ice in the glass.

"Jules has had a busy day," my father said, smiling.

"Oh, really," my mother responded, passing my father his highball. "I think he looks pale. What can the matter be?"

FIVE

...

The morning of my road exam, I woke up in a sweat.

I had forgotten to stop at the cash machine to get $100 to tip the driver instructor if, and when, I passed my road exam. (*Tip:* from the abbreviation for "to insure promptness," or so said the caption to a *New Yorker* cartoon I once read.) We were meant to be off in an hour.

And I had dreamt about driving again; when the highway rose too superiorly near Goldenrod, I could not clear my eyes of some obscurity. I struggled with the steering wheel; I awakened with the alarm. I turned on the television: the Princess of Wales was unhappy again; a young mother was murdered by a stray bullet in Spanish Harlem. There had been a light rain and a few more triborough slayings.

It had been arranged, and reconfirmed the evening before, by the manager of the McCaulay's Driving School for a fellow named Hector, an instructor whom I had not yet met, to pick me up in a McCaulay's car at 7:30; the road exam was scheduled for 9 A.M. Even in the worst traffic, ninety minutes would allow plenty of time to get to Sheepshead Bay, I had been promised.

What to wear? To excuse any error in driving I might commit, or problem I might present, I decided to dress up out of respect for all the examiners at the Motor Vehicle Department; I'm not certain I can explain this logic. I showered and shaved and put on a blue Giorgio Armani suit, a red for success tie, and was ready twenty minutes before Hector was due to arrive. Just enough time to rush to the cash machine and back, which I did. At 7:25 I returned to my insufficiently furnished – one desk, one chair, one bed, two TVs – one-bedroom apartment on the fourth floor of an East Seventies brownstone and waited. At 7:30 there was no sign of Hector, nor any hint of his arrival ten minutes later.

The phone rang. "Julian Orr?" a man's voice asked.

"Yes," I answered.

"This is Hector; I'm not coming."

"What do you mean?" I pleaded.

"Can't make it," Hector grumbled and hung up.

Red alert, red alert, what to do? Have I sufficiently explained the equal measures of anxiety and desperation that surrounded this lively exercise of learning to drive and getting a license? The therapist was after me to attain closure on the past – and nothing less – for which the possession of a driver's license and a trip to my parents' graves was the ultimate, sweeping movement in this symphony of psychiatry. And, as I think I already mentioned, my friends were sick of my talking about learning to drive; I agreed: I could expend all this energy in more practical pursuits, like learning to cook or meeting deadlines early. I grabbed the phone and dialed McCaulay's, only to hear a voice-mail message at the other end saying the academy – academy? – opened for business at 9 A.M., the hour scheduled for my road test.

Too late. I left an uppity, menacing message nonetheless.

I paced; I called McCaulay's back just in case someone was there. At 8 A.M., with but an hour left before my road test was meant to take place, I took a taxi to the driving "academy," slumped on a sunless street in the East Eighties. I banged on the door; nobody was there. I fretted. I paced up and down the sidewalk. I crossed the street and paced in front of a little stationery shop, which actually housed the office of a well-known escort service. A woman wearing a green satin suit and black stiletto pumps exited the shop and got into a waiting radio taxi. She smelled of gardenias and rouge.

I walked to the southeast corner of Lexington Avenue and bought a copy of the newspaper in which I penned my daily drivel; I actually couldn't remember what copy I had filed for that day. On page ten was the column and its news that a tycoon had acquired a Sargent painting that was too big for his Park Avenue parlor so he had fired his art dealer, and news that the owner of Winston's, the favorite society eatery, had been given a new pug dog for the occasion of his seventieth birthday . . . like that. To buy the time away from my desk to take today's road test I planned to file the first interview with the aforementioned dog in which said pooch—channeled by Winston's curmudgeonly owner—spoke of his position as head mascot of society's most preferred watering hole. There was a rough draft of the column already on file in my computer.

Gilded latchkey children scampered by toward any one of several private schools in the area; two Asian women in dark cocktail suits entered the office of the escort service. Humidity took hold of the morning air and the day turned the colors of a rat's back; I spied the manager of McCaulay's making his approach toward the school and ambushed him at the door with my tale.

This tallish man of about fifty in a brown suit said nothing. He unlocked the McCaulay's door, and I followed him inside, all the while emitting a litany of complaints, pleas, and accusations: Where is Hector, how could this happen, how could I ever recommend McCaulay's to my friends, how could McCaulay's ever again in good faith proclaim itself on matchbooks, and, remembering the current, popular, psycho-business babble of the day, how were we going to "get to win" on this matter?

The McCaulay's manager stripped the lid off a Styrofoam cup of coffee and sipped. We stood in a dreary place: a dull, green-painted classroom with school desks and images on the walls of car crashes and signs warning against the perils of drinking while under the influence. "I don't think you understand," I pleaded. "If I don't get my license today, my driver's permit will expire before we can arrange for another test. Then I will have to go through this whole, goddamn process again, and it won't be at McCaulay's."

He listened; he didn't seem to care.

I brought out the fancy ammunition now: "Did I mention," I warned, affecting calm, "that I intend to write about my experience of learning to drive? This is the, what, second time McCaulay's has failed me in my efforts? Not a great endorsement for the school for my article, would you say?"

Not attractive on my part, of course, but it got his attention. "I'll call Hector and see what I can do," he said.

I went outside and waited on the stoop. An early spring sun knifed through the gray and humid day; I waited. I returned indoors.

"Hector will be here in a few minutes," the McCaulay's manager promised. "There has been a misunderstanding, but we will get you to your road test in time."

"Really? Can we really get to Sheepshead Bay by nine? You said yesterday to allow an hour and a half."

"Sure, sure, don't worry," the manager of the driving school said, sipping his coffee and leafing through a pile of papers.

There wasn't much I could do but trust him. We waited for Hector; the manager of the driving school began to ask me about several local celebrities and became rather animated. Did I know Donald Trump, he wondered.

"Do I know Donald Trump?" I answered and rehashed whatever tidbits I could remember as we waited for Hector.

SIX

. . .

Through the windows of my parents' bedroom, which I shared with my father, one could see, especially that summer, a grand weeping willow tree. With its gently lashing branches and sweeping leaves, this tree was one of the highlights of our neighborhood; enacting swinging scenes from *Tarzan* was a popular game with the children. Sometimes we would just comb the leaves with our hands as if they were hair.

One early morning that summer, I lay in bed next to my father and watched the tree flutter, its leaves like faint green tears, thinking of nothing but that. I was waiting for my parents to awaken and for another of our almost perfectly speechless days to begin. Then, like the cars that had crashed a few nights before, another sound came new to me; from the room where my mother slept a sudden choking noise as if machinery iron were spitting, ripping.

I shook my father awake. We ran to my mother. It was hot as a furnace in her room. My mother lay in bed convulsing, her eyes flared opened by fright and drowning in tears. Her chest heaved up, down. Her bedclothes were wet and torn apart; her night-gown was transparent with sweat, her green eyes red with alarm.

My mother could not speak, but from deep within her came sounds of something wrong and breaking.

My father cried. "Leah," he called her by her name. "Leah! Leah!"

I don't remember what happened immediately next. In a span of time that I feel was very long but understand couldn't have been, an ambulance arrived. My father's thought had been to lock me in the bathroom so I would not see; was I crying again? There were sirens and yelling and footsteps; from the bathroom window I saw my mother carried on a stretcher covered with starched white sheets. My father followed; his hands covered his face. The ambulance door closed.

I felt like a balloon imploded; my life let out. Hands grabbing the windowsill, I watched my parents go away. Instead of fright I experienced confirmation: something I had always feared came true.

The bathroom door opened; there stood Aunt Libby, my mother's sister. At other times bright and as perfectly drawn as a fashion illustration in the Sunday paper, she now seemed as frail as a future of ash.

"My mother's having a baby?" I asked. I can hear myself now, a cheerful dish of strawberries and buttercups, imagining that only the arrival of a much pined-for sibling would set this morning right.

"Ask your father," Aunt Libby answered, taking me by the hand.

When, hours later, my father returned home, I asked just that. "Jules," he said, "oh, Jules."

"Is she, is she?"

"Yes," he sighed and shook his head no.

I chased the last bit of sunset into the neighborhood; I landed next door, where, on the lawn of my best friend Michael's house, he and his brother, Bobby, were playing baseball. It seemed almost every year their mother, Mrs. Grosvenor, was having a baby, and it always seemed a mystery that excluded me; they were a family of six siblings with plenty of relations, too.

"My mother's having a baby," I said as Bobby threw the baseball toward his younger brother's bat.

"Is not, Jules," Michael said, hitting the ball without effort.

"Is too," I said.

"Is not," Michael said, hitting another ball.

"Is too, is too!" I insisted, near tears.

"Is not, is not!" Michael yelled.

Darkness fell; our banter continued. I was eight years old, screaming make-believes on another summer's night. "She's dying," Michael said. Mrs. Grosvenor rushed from her kitchen. The screen door crashed behind her. She put her arm around me and pulled me close. "Everything will be all right. Everything will be all right," she repeated. "Michael, go put some of my Toll House cookies in a bag for Jules to take home, please."

We fumbled in our house without my mother. Aunt Libby came every night and prepared our meal. My father and she spoke little; I might ask about the baby—he was a boy, I determined—and my father and aunt would slouch into a familial silence.

About ten days later, I was playing on the lawn when a limousine curled up the driveway. In the back seat I saw my mother, frail and colorless, her head resting on my father's shoulder. When she got out of the car and walked head down into the house, she was not holding a baby, nor was my father.

I walked to the boundaries of our lawn, where the evergreen trees separated us from the road and the house of the neighbors, and sat in silence on the grass. The neighbors came to see my mother and say hello and whisper their best wishes and concerns.

I looked up. Michael was there. "I learned how to tie my shoes today," he said without bragging. "Let me teach you," he offered.

We sat and practiced making bows while the house filled with a society of courtesy. Oh, yes, I was sad, like the child who finds a starfish at the shore and drops it in the sand when he meant it for his pocket; he retraces his steps and looks and looks and never finds the only treasure he can that day imagine. From there, tomorrow comes.

SEVEN

...

This must be Hector now, I thought.

A McCaulay's car came coughing down the street; on the roof of the dingy Dodge was a sign, same graphics as those on the matchbooks, advertising the school.

"Here's Hector," said the manager of the driving school. I followed him to the street. He stepped up to the driver's side window and had a few words with his employee. My first take on Hector was that he was handsome, and I felt thoroughly inappropriate for having that thought. Hector and the driving school manager bantered back and forth; although I couldn't quite hear what they said, I got the impression Hector was not happy.

"Good luck," the manager said, opening the passenger's door to the driving school car for me. Dripping sweat from an outfit of spandex that wrapped him like so many rolls of sausage, some fool nearly knocked us over as he sped by on new Rollerblades.

Before I seated myself amid yesterday's Dunkin' Donut bags and Styrofoam coffee cups, I gently raised the trousers of my Armani suit, which I had seen gentlemen do to ward off unflattering creases. Hector met this sartorial indulgence with a leer; as alluring as his dark eyes were, I thought they also seemed a bit unfocused.

"Are you sure we can get there in time?" I asked the manager as I got into the car.

"Yes, yes; Hector will take care of you," he answered and closed the door with such gusto I felt vacuum-packed inside the Dodge.

"How are you today?" I asked Hector, trying to win a friend with robust jauntiness. "Ready for Sheepshead Bay?"

Hector coiled his cherry lower lip and turned the engine on; we shot toward the corner and ran a red light. It was 8:20 A.M. He propped up on the dashboard a crumpled piece of paper; in pencil were scribbled directions to the Motor Vehicle office in Sheepshead Bay—out of the way, or simply unknown, for McCaulay's Driving School instructors, who frequented the MV in Yonkers.

Hector squinted at the paper; we banged and bounced our way east toward the FDR Drive. I'd learned enough at McCaulay's to know that Hector was driving recklessly. "Do you really think we can get there in time?" I asked.

From a pack rolled in the sleeve of his T-shirt, he squeezed out a Winston cigarette and positioned it in his mouth. He groped about in his pants pocket for a lighter and struggled to target the flame to the cigarette.

"Papa! Papa! *Atención!*" came a girl's voice from the back seat.

"Fuck you, cunts! *Puta, puta!*" Hector yelled, exhaling smoke as a mother and child jumped out of our way.

Cowering in the corner on the seat behind Hector, I saw for the first time that morning a pretty little girl about seven or eight years old. Wearing a pink dress and black patent leather shoes, she looked as if she was going to a party, but she hardly seemed pleased about it; she was on the verge of tears. Not that I blamed her; Hector's speed-up–slow-down driving and near hits and misses had begun to terrify me, too.

"What's your name?" I asked.

She shriveled into herself; she did not answer.

"What's your stuffed animal's name?" I asked about a furry thing she clutched in her arms.

Hector led us toward the highway; sun had lightened the gray city sky so it had all the dull and greasy brightness of fried eggs.

"Does your daughter—the little girl is your daughter, I assume—does she not speak English?" I asked Hector.

He stubbed his cigarette out in the ashtray—actually, he missed the ashtray and hit its rim, so cinders fell on the car floor.

Hector did not answer. What to do? This certainly was not the time for me to trot out my boarding school Spanish, about as good as that of an American lady I once knew in Spain who, on the cook's day off, took great pride in her ability to do the grocery shopping herself. "Give-o mio a head-o of lettucio," she would instruct the grocer.

So I just sat there, watching my watch and hoping Hector's rodeo driving could get us to the Motor Vehicle Department in time for my test. You feel the speed of cheap cars in your stomach; as the Dodge belched toward the Belt Parkway I became nauseated. Hector felt for the radio dial, and soon the sounds of the local Latino station came blasting at full volume. I was bouncing around so much in my seat due to the speed with which the driving school instructor took a curve or hit the brake, I felt like Carmen Miranda, bound, gagged, but still performing. Hector's daughter curled herself nearly into a ball and did not look out the car windows.

Today we die, I thought. I was glad I had secreted a cellular phone in the pocket of my suit jacket; it would come in handy when the first tire blew. At 8:50 A.M., just ten minutes before my road test, we were nowhere near our destination. Hector squinted, yelled, slapped the steering wheel, fiddled with the radio volume and spit obscenities at most everyone on the roadway. His storm, his tempest. We surfed what I understood was the Belt Parkway. Looping and lost in circles we left the highway, we rode the streets, we got back on another highway. We passed a prison. We passed mail trucks, limousines, abandoned vans broken down along the roadside. We passed a truck hauling beauty products and a rest stop where the drivers of cars and trucks disappeared behind drought-dried trees to pee. We passed teenagers cutting school, salesmen, motorcyclists, an ambulance driver puffing on a joint, and mostly we passed men. We passed other men in other cars ashened like ours by city soot.

And, when all lanes met in a grand traffic jam, we communed with concrete; without the sounds of speed the radio was deafening. We didn't move; we couldn't move. It was a dead stop. At 9:02 A.M., 9:03, 9:04, 9:05, 9:06, 9:07, 9:08, 9:09, 9:10, 9:11, 9:12, 9:13, 9:14 . . . a dead stop with sambas. When we moved again at 9:15, Hector, who seemed to be having trouble reading the instructions he'd been given, pulled into a gas station and asked the attendant for directions.

"You don't know where we are going, do you?" I said to Hector when we were back on the road.

He looked at me and sneered. He spit at me and yelled, "Faggot!" slamming his fist into my stomach for punctuation. Of course it hurt, but how did he know? It had taken *me* years to figure it out.

EIGHT

...

Did I mention that my father
sold cars? That he was born in Russia in 1895 and came to America,
to Goldenrod, in 1900 and sold tires, and later tires and Pontiacs?

He was already of a certain age when he married my mother
and they had me; he was sixty and she was forty when I was
born. For both, it was a first marriage; they were the oldest
children in their families, and it had been their jobs to see to it
that their younger siblings were college educated and married
before they could consider going out on their own. Although they
had never met, my father was aware of my mother, and his
inquiries about her eventually led to their introduction by a
mutual friend. Or at least that is what my mother told me once;
another time, when she was well into her illness, she told me my
father had loved a woman who was not Jewish. The woman had
gotten pregnant, and, my mother said, my paternal grandfather
banished her with a large check to northern California, where she
had a son. Perhaps my second trip after I learned to drive should
be to head west to find my long-lost brother.

That summer, in 1962, I remember a morning a few days
after my mother returned home from the hospital without a baby.

I was sitting on the grass, on our soldiering green lawn a grave-yard of blades, when my father approached dangling the keys to his car. In his other hand he carried a brown suitcase.

"Jules," my father said, "we are going for a ride."

It was our way; I was always ready for a ride. My mother, still frail after her stay in the hospital, opened the door to the back porch; she was in mid-speech. "No, Saul, no, Saul; this is wrong," she said.

My grandfather looked gray as an old man wrapped in ghosts. He walked toward the car. My father raised his hand, to silence my mother. From bits of conversation I'd overheard, I knew that my grandfather was going to live in something called an old-age home. Perhaps it was a new invention; my father would like that. He would think that it was good, and right, and the very place for an old man, which my grandfather was, an American temple for a man who had arrived in the promised land with just a few gold bricks and more posture than promise. I think my father took to heart everything American, like this old-age home, but why did he separate his parents? My grandmother drifted in the shadows behind my mother and sobbed.

My father wore a blue and white seersucker suit jacket and brown pants and shoes. He drove his father and myself through the summer day in a red Pontiac station wagon to West Hartford, about ninety minutes away. I sat in the back seat and focused on the car's motion; my grandfather sat in the passenger seat next to my father and shook his head, "No, no, no."

"Jules," my father said, his hands piloting the steering wheel, "sing your grandfather a song."

"Zayde," I said, "a song?"

"Please don't sing," my grandfather whispered.

"No, Pa; Jules should sing. Sing, Jules."

I only knew one song, one I'd learned in school. "He's Got the Whole World in His Hands," I sang with all my might. I remember singing the song and looking out the window waiting for the time I could stop singing, as we turned into the driveway of the old-age home. Behind black, wrought-iron gates was a mansion. Over the door was a gilded sign that read "Hebrew Home for the Aged." Strangers in white coats came in waves to meet the car; they took the suitcase, they enveloped my grandfather.

"I'll visit every Sunday, Pa," my father promised.

And he was gone, although my father did visit every Sunday. My uncles persuaded my father to let my grandmother reside with my grandfather at the old-age home. My grandfather died that winter. As it often happens with couples who have been together for so long, my grandmother died only a few months later.

We sat still in the Pontiac in front of the old-age home for a few minutes before my father turned on the ignition. "Have you ever driven a car?" my father asked.

My father settled me on his lap. "To drive, Jules, you put your hands at a position of ten-to-two as if the steering wheel was a clock. You look both ways and drive with caution, especially when you are driving with girls."

We snaked down the drive from the mansion toward the highway. I could not see well over the wheel; the car sloped toward the road like milk dripped from a waxed carton. I was frightened of the car, scared it would slide out of control.

"But you mustn't be frightened," my father said. "A car is like a horse; if it smells fear, it attacks."

I wanted to die.

"Keep your hands at ten-to-two on the wheel, Jules," my father repeated. "My foot is near the brake, don't worry. Now lead the car toward the gate. Turn the wheel to the right . . . "

Very near to the gate an ambulance—no sirens—turned into the driveway, bearing, I assumed, the next grandfather for the Hebrew Home for the Aged. Instead of turning the wheel to the right as I had been told, I turned it to the left and nearly collided with the ambulance. My father applied the brakes to the Pontiac; we jolted forward. The driver of the ambulance jumped from his seat and cursed my father; he bounced me back into the passenger's seat. I tried not to cry. I turned the radio on; my father turned it off. I cried; my father raised and pressed a callused index finger to my lips. I smelled his work—the garage, gasoline, oil cloths, the mechanics' cigarettes—and his lime-scented after-shave.

My father drove. The gate to the Hebrew Home for the Aged had two proud, gilded Stars of David bright as torches. We were back on the road heading home, not many clouds in the sky. I wanted to sit back in my father's lap. I asked if I might try driving again. He suggested I sing instead.

"A song, sir?" I whispered.

"That nice song about the whole world in his hands, Jules."

I sang; the world waited. Isn't that the state of childhood until it ends?

NINE

. . .

The savvy New Yorker comes to understand that, alas, sooner or later he or she will entertain his fifteen minutes of violence.

So that morning as we looped the roadways of Manhattan, and Hector's fists punched my ribs and his hands with marble knuckles slammed my face against the window of the driving school Dodge, I told myself everything but certain wounds could be mended by plastic surgery; you are almost contractually obliged to be optimistic about such things when you work for a fashion magazine. I told myself to relax; I prayed he did not have a knife. "Relax, relax," I told myself. This morning I was falling from a building but, with cosmic concentration, I could land soft as a cat. How many lives were left?

"Papa! Papa! *Atención*," Hector's daughter begged repeatedly from her unprotected nest in the back seat. She was right; with all the pounding on me, Hector had gone completely blind to the gray, unexitable road.

Hector's calling me "faggot" was now upgraded to "fucking faggot" and then this: he would get off the highway, drive across the bridge to the corresponding entrance ramp, and get back on

45

the road again. As terrifying as these orbits were, they were maddening also; you knew it wouldn't end well, but when? And there seemed little point in my trying to poke him in the eyes; Hector was bigger and quicker.

Obviously, I had triggered rage in him. We were at the height of the movement for political correctness that season. As a devoted liberal, I thought, and still do think, it is completely polite to avoid semantical offenses to any group of people whose difficulties have nothing to do with any lack of effort on their part. What had I done to offend him, I wondered. I squeezed my brain, so to speak, to divine some explanations; the Dodge hurled like a comet from exit to entrance ramp.

Hector lived in Spanish Harlem—the McCaulay's Driving School manager had said so—where children were daily killed by stray bullets and no one outside his community cared. I lived in a neighborhood where if one was tripped by an intruder it made front-page news. Hector came from a world where, I assumed, machismo was important. I lived in a community so hypothetically sophisticated that I could say in print that I had been out so long it looked like in to me, and my employers published those sentiments and hid their personal discomfort under a matrix of corporate acceptance. Hector, who was at least ten years younger than me, probably was already pressed against the so-called glass ceiling of job opportunities; despite his good looks I sarcastically submit that I somehow doubted he was in the right place to become Madonna's next all-star Hispanic boyfriend. I, on the other hand, was white and professionally mobile for the most part as long as I did not venture too far from what is known as "the creative fields," where urban homosexuals are safely planted, as well as sometimes defeated, by the duplicities of acceptance.

All my life, I think where I've gone wrong is in wanting things too much, like my driver's license. Had I pushed too hard? Was I overstimulated by my therapist? So I'd begin again. My parents would always be buried in the cemetery. What's another year without a visit from me? None of us are going anywhere really.

I almost said, "Hector, I'm sorry. Let's go home." But I was distracted.

On the radio blared the Gipsy Kings' version of Frank Sinatra's song "My Way." Hector barely avoided sideswiping a bleached blond in a brown Corvette; his daughter screamed, saying something, I thought I understood with my limited Spanish, about his eyes, or was it her eyes? I didn't know. Her father squinted in the rearview mirror; it was obvious he loved her. I decided to appeal to this love, to anoint our unholy threesome with a potion of general concern for the well-being of an innocent child, and said: "I feel sorry for your daughter."

Hector grabbed my left cheek and slammed my head against the window to my right. "I know where you live; I'll come kill you, motherfucking-cocksucker-faggot, if you ever, ever, threaten my daughter. Do you understand, faggot!? Answer me!"

I couldn't; his next fist into my ribs knocked the air out of me. Hector's daughter cried; she tore at the ribbon in her hair. I understood that my comment had sounded menacing to Hector. He thought because he never got me to my driving test I would retaliate by – what? – getting him fired. That without employment he would not be able to feed his daughter. That is what Hector had determined from me. It also occurred to me that, given his machismo, in front of his daughter he wanted as much as I did to get to the Motor Vehicle Department on time.

Hector flattened his palm against my cheek, ground my head into the passenger's window, and pumped the gas pedal of the Dodge. I'd been zapped by competitors, and probably got them back, but I had never really been anyone's enemy before; I certainly was Hector's. For whatever thousand reasons I could barely think of in my exhausted state, I blew his fuse, and here I was—the boy who went to dancing school and spent his adult life at perfume launches—one lost man's Hitler. I wanted to go home; I was dizzy. Sure: click your Armani heels together, and you are still thundering on the Belt Parkway.

"Listen, Hector," I muttered, trying to move my lips against his callused palm, "I am not your enemy. I'm sorry if I came across testy; it's just that I would really have liked to get my license this year. There's someplace I wanted to drive to, and I was stressed out by the idea of taking the test. I'm sorry; can't we go home now?"

A yellow school bus cut in front of us; Hector slammed his brakes. The driver of the school bus saluted us with a raised bottle of beer; Hector gave him the finger.

"Fuck you, faggot! Fuck you!" Hector bellowed at me over the radio sounds. He hit his fastest speed yet on the road—where were the police?—and zigzagged out of control. He tried to open my door and push me out, but I had locked it; his arm wasn't long enough to reach the lock behind me. He slapped my head forward against the dashboard and then back against the headrest. The gesture was repeated; this time we nearly hit a nursery truck stocked with evergreens and were momentarily confined in a highway island of traffic.

"Suck this, motherfucker, suck this cock; your mouth big enough, faggot? Fuck you, you're not good enough to suck my dick!" Hector yelled, one hand jangling his crotch, the other on the steering wheel or aimed at me.

Hector's daughter hid on the floor of the Dodge. The back of her father's hand, upon which I could detect the last remnants of drugstore after-shave, fanned against my lip. The first blood of the morning dripped like sundae fudge over my chin and onto my white dress shirt. "Help, help!" I screamed, but why bother?

When does this day end, I wondered.

TEN

. . .

My mother did not approve of most people, including one of the girls in our neighborhood, named Dana Deamour.

Dana was sixteen when I was eight, and always sixteen as I remember her; her mother, Esther, worked in a shoe factory, and her grandmother, known only as Mrs. Stanley, cleaned house for my mother. The three women lived on the west end of Terry Avenue, which was the street at the back of our house; theirs was a small place with a tilted porch, the result of a summer storm, one of many that I can recall when I was growing up.

"Mrs. Stanley is a wonderful woman," I remember my mother said often, "but Dana, well, there's trouble brewing there, and why not? Her father is poor white trash."

It didn't get any worse than that: calling someone poor white trash. The only thing worse, I think, was that the first time I heard my mother use the expression, I knew instantly what she meant. Poor white trash meant the neighbors who drank beer instead of highballs on their porches. They were women with blond hair and dark roots; they were people who wore thin, cotton clothes washed gray regardless of their original color. They were people with lost fathers; they were people who had sex.

I worshiped Dana as if she were a princess. Her blond ponytail was the thickest in her high school class. Despite what my mother said, I think she was a good student. Her after-school job was tutoring me in arithmetic; she could add, subtract, and talk about troll dolls, which were the rage then, as they are again now, at the same time looking out the window like she expected someone to come tapping at the sill with a red rose. Dana adored the movies, she went to matinees in town almost every Saturday afternoon, and she said as soon as she could she would get herself to California. "It's where the boys are, Jules," she laughed. "It's where I bet my father is," she added.

No one actually knew where Dana's father was; I had asked my mother, and she shrugged with disapproval and said she hadn't a clue. Sometimes, however, Dana would surprise us with some new present she had received; she'd tell everyone it was a gift from her father, that he had sent it to her—most recently that summer a new pair of roller skates.

"Where is your father?" Mrs. Stanley wanted to know.

I was visiting Dana at her house one afternoon when she showed her grandmother her new skates. "I don't know where he is, but he sent me these; aren't they just wonderful?"

"From where did he send them?" Mrs. Stanley insisted. "He didn't send them to this house, did he? How could he? I would have seen the mailman bring the box."

"He sent them to me, Nanna, that's all you need to know. He sent them to me. Isn't that enough?" Dana answered.

They fought. I thought it was wonderful the way Dana received these presents from a father no one else could find.

Around that time that summer everyone in the neighborhood was talking about storms, about hurricanes. There came a point every summer when we could have a hurricane every day, I think, for at least a week or two. You'd hear about them on the radio, or on the television, and everyone rushed about preparing against the storms, putting masking tape across their windows, worrying about their trees, my father his roses.

My mother's reaction to all the concern was to take a contrary position. "Let it rain, let it storm, let this old house come down, Saul," she'd say.

"Leah, please," my father scolded. He was thinking about putting sandbags at the feet of his roses.

I sat in front of our old Zenith radio and listened to a faceless man give voice to a hurricane's progress. Its arrival was narrated inch by inch as the trees lashed and the blades of grass twisted and the sky went muddy and fell with rain. My parents would sit beside me; my father turned the radio off for fear lightning would come through the Zenith and strike me. Instead of feeling safe then, I felt homesick. I thought about the movies when the monster comes and families run in the streets and lose their children; I remembered a book read to us at school the previous winter called *The Boy and His Friend the Blizzard*. It told the story of a boy who lost his mother in a blizzard; he looked and looked for her until the blizzard became his mother and they were one in the snow.

My mother lighted a cigarette and exhaled smoke in rings. She ran her hand through her auburn hair and sighed.

"My roses," my father said, worried. Instead of putting sandbags at their roots he had tied them with black tape to their stakes.

"Saul, stop worrying about the roses," my mother said.

"But my roses, Leah," he repeated.

The radio was turned off; the storm came in a line like a horse tail at full chase. It blew everything east; through the window we saw Dana Deamour zoom down Terry Avenue on her new roller skates.

"My God, Saul, did you see her?"

"Dana Deamour on roller skates?" My father couldn't believe it.

"She'll kill herself," my mother said. "She'll hit a car; she'll hit a tree. A tree will hit her. I'm calling Mrs. Stanley."

But the phones were dead.

Dana Deamour wore cut-off blue jeans rolled high at her thighs and a white shirt knotted above her waist; her blond hair, with its dark roots, wasn't in a ponytail, not for this ride. It was loose as a devil's wings. The wind blew her east; she was smiling.

They found Dana under an elm tree at the bottom of a hill on Main Street. She was burrowed in the tree's ancient roots, soaked to the bone. They took her home; she was crying. Dana Deamour spent the next days in bed with a fever. She cried things no one understood. Everyone felt sorry; there was some talk whispered about a baby. Dana Deamour rested; the skates were ruined. They weren't really a present from her father but from someone else, someone Dana found while she was looking for the first man who escaped.

The sun shined again; my parents drank highballs in cut crystal glasses on the porch during the cocktail hour. Mrs. Stanley and Dana's mother, Esther, visited. My father made extra highballs and surveyed his garden. "I think the roses will come back," he told everyone. Most of the roses had blown in Dana Deamour's direction, but you could still find a few petals on our lawn.

"Besides everything else, Dana needs eyeglasses," Mrs. Stanley told us.

"They'll ruin her looks," my mother said.

ELEVEN

...

The line to the end starts here,
The line to the end starts here,
Here is where we started; here is where we parted.
At the beginning of the end of the line, dear, at the
beginning of the end of the line, dear.

Friends at the end of the line, dear?
Friends if we pretend, dear, now at the beginning of our
end, dear.

Don't worry, I know I'm certainly not a poet, although I write poems, usually in cocktail lounges, which usually is where love ends. Meaning, love, or a reasonable facsimile, ends, because you wanted too much, and you go to a cocktail lounge and order a drink, and, by the second round, you're writing poetry on damp paper napkins and remembering all your relationships and, mostly, your youth: when you were young and you loved love.

I wrote the above little ditty when I stopped romanticizing a symphony between myself and a drummer I'd met at a charity ball. About three years ago, the big breakup, which really was nothing but another day's whimper, sometime between getting my learner's permit to drive and failing to get to my road test on time.

"I'm tired. Can't we go home please," I murmured, hoping Hector might be tired, too.

He wasn't; he drove faster but not toward home. We zigzagged; we got off one ramp and back on another. My lip still bled but at a slower drool. The radio blasted. Hector's daughter had gotten up from the car floor and was curled in the back seat. Was this escapade going to go on all day? When would Hector hit me again? Maybe I should just jump out of the car and see what happened. Conditioned to think like a shrink, I wondered how I had gotten into this fix.

As Hector sped the Dodge in his random, rodeo way, I interviewed myself, questions I might ask a person in my situation if I was assigned to cover the story for which the headline would read: "Upper East Side writer abducted by driving school teacher" or "Driving school teacher infuriated by Upper East Side writer murders in social self-defense."

The answers to the interview, in no special order, included:

He hates you.

He wants to kill you.

You instigated it; it's the Armani suit.

You created this situation; you didn't want to get your driver's license. (Yes, I do; I want to go home.)

New York is a battlefield between the haves and the have-nots.

He wants to fuck you.

You've come on to him.

He is crazy. You are crazier.

He's on steroids? He's on drugs?

He wants to fuck you; he wants to fuck you dead.

Today is but another in a series of endless upsets designed in an elaborate system of self-sabotage that prohibits you on a regular basis from meeting your newspaper column deadline at two o'clock each weekday afternoon.

There's more to Hector's rage than you will ever know or could possibly understand.

Jump from the Dodge now and suffer your slashes; everything can be repaired by a good plastic surgeon.

"Faggot," Hector said, spitting. The dribble stuck to my left cheek.

I looked out the window; everything was still a hurricane of cars, and they each told the New York story of haves and have-nots. This was my soapbox about cars in New York: people with the most money drove chauvinistically tarted-up Jeeps; not only were the Range Rover and Mercedes varieties remarkably expensive, they took up a lot of space, which is the measure of status in New York. There were the littler cars for the littler people, I supposed, and then there were the taxis, where New York's penchant for racism is most manifested. Most taxi drivers are immigrants from some third world country who can barely speak English; they rarely know quite how to get to where their passengers want to go. Ever hostile to first-generation newcomers, New York, a city of newcomers, has institutionalized its bigotry by allowing strangers to take jobs as taxi drivers without sufficient preparation. Although you don't quite know who is the slave to whom during a bad taxi ride, the person in the back seat, regardless of how sweetly demeaned he might be elsewhere, will emit a foulness of spirit comparable only to certain landowners in the Civil War. Even though most taxi drivers drive like criminals, it was society that prepared the crime.

La!

It was 10:30 A.M. Hector squinted into the sunlight; I tried to see how much gas was left in the tank, but when I leaned over, he slapped my head back. Despite myself, I realized Hector was almost a pretty man; I tried to imagine him as a little boy, before whatever made him so angry had happened. I couldn't see it; instead, I saw the muscular arms revealed by his tight, white T-shirt and felt defeated, frightened, exhausted. A lock of his thick black hair vibrated on his forehead as we chased direction-less on the highway. I noticed that he was bruised at the top of his Roman-shaped nose; something had hit him recently between the eyes, and only recently. It wasn't me, of course. A small bit of blood was crusted in his left nostril.

"You've been bleeding," I said quietly, too weak to speak louder than the radio.

After a disdainful, long-lasting stare, Hector banged my head against the car window—again—and punched me in the ribs. His daughter screamed, but the hits didn't hurt as much as they had at first. Perhaps I'd gone numb; all I knew was that I was so tired, and that my editor was never going to believe this even if I did manage to get out of this car in order to file copy today.

Around and around we drove; I was so tired. Sometimes, and this was one of them, I could only wonder what I might have accomplished had I not always been so awfully tired.

TWELVE

...

"Jules, wake up," my father said, leaning over me in our bed.

"Daddy?"

"Wake up, Jules. We're going for a ride."

I found my mother in the kitchen wearing a new navy blue dress with a white collar. Looking out the window over the sink at nothing but the summer day, she drank coffee and smoked a cigarette. Mrs. Stanley helped me dress; I wore, with certain embarrassment, a sailor suit—blue top and britches—freshly arrived from the department store in Hartford. My father wore a brown suit; I followed him and my mother to one of the Pontiacs parked in the driveway.

"Where are we going?" I asked.

"Not very far," my mother answered.

Driving to the other side of town, we came to a large white house that I recognized from other rides; it was where my mother was born and raised. The house was owned now by friends of my parents; there were quite a few cars parked in the driveway and along the street. We walked to the front door; inside the house were people also very dressed up for a typical summer's day.

Goldenrod's rabbi, a tall thin man with gray hair and a nose like a heron's beak, was there; so, too, was the cantor, shaped like a penguin, standing next to him. A third man, whom I did not know, completed the trio; they all wore white, fringed prayer shawls and yarmulkes. They hovered over something; I didn't know what until it cried.

The people of the house, their name was Black, had recently had a son, a first child. The rabbi, the cantor, the other man surrounded the baby; its mother greeted us with a serene, soundless smile. The baby cried.

"Jules," my father said, handing me a yarmulke, "put this on and keep it on."

My parents mingled. I found an ottoman and sat; the yarmulke kept falling off, I kept putting it back on. It was like playing a solitaire game of Simon Says, and I was losing. No one seemed to notice. An older lady, round in a polka dot dress, bent over and squeezed my cheek. "Cute," she said, as if she were assessing a violet plant. "Whose are you?" Her breath smelled of smoked salmon.

I pointed toward my parents.

"How nice," she said. "I thought from the way you are dressed you might be a little sailor washed ashore." She walked away; the yarmulke slipped off my head again.

The guests had stampeded toward the rabbi and the baby; he shrieked. Glasses clinked; the boy was circumcised. His mother walked toward me with the baby in her arms. "Wouldn't you like to hold our son?" she asked. The baby, wrapped in a fine, cotton blanket, was delivered into my arms. The yarmulke fell from my head; my father looked disappointed. The baby was not given to me to hold in any capricious manner; all the women in the room seemed to bend with his mother toward me. Someone took our picture. My mother, standing at the other side of the parlor, lighted a cigarette and waved to me.

At first, I was surprised by what it felt like to hold the baby; it seemed to me his weight was illogically distributed. He was all head. I looked into his eyes, and I started to cry; rather than being pleased, why did holding a baby make me feel so lonely? The child was swept away immediately, and my father was left with the business of consoling me publicly. "Go outside and wait in the car," he said. "We'll be going home soon."

As ever, I did as I was told.

THIRTEEN

...

Always two thoughts, a mantra of sentimentality: I want to go home; I wish my parents were here. Because of the differences in our ages, they always seemed far away from me, certainly compared to other children's parents. And after my parents died, the initial distance between us compounded our differences year after year; do I remember them fairly, accurately? My memory of childhood is like a found school notebook covered in dust. Scraped clean it reveals that the lessons have been altered, erased.

I shivered, although it was warm enough in the McCaulay's Driving School Dodge. The wild ride continued; the radio played and if I did not move or sigh, Hector did not hit me. We whirled around the highway, nearly colliding with other cars, and I interviewed myself more.

Q: Whom do you love?

A: I loved my father, then he died. I loved my mother, then she died.

Q: Did you kill them?

A: I suppose. I loved them, then they died.

Q: It's your fault?

A: Who else's?

Hector screamed a wordless roar and floored the accelerator—*whoosh*. I closed my eyes and thought about romance; I don't know why. But right now there was in me this desire for another with whom I might dance and spin and plan again. Come into me / and press your heart against my heart / a seashell we will find in the dancing, always dancing, sand / A surprise / a highway ahead of blue lines and white circles / the seashell on your forehead the emblem of this our eternal love.

"I am going to kill you, faggot," Hector said, still getting us nowhere on the highway.

Hector's daughter had taken the ribbon out of her hair and stuffed it in her mouth, to stop herself from screaming, I supposed. Funny, I thought, in the world I write about, they put on fancy dresses and go every night to parties that are so loud no one could hear anyone scream even if one felt it was the most authentic social act left.

"So kill me," I muttered.

"You want me to kill you, don't you, faggot?" Hector yelled.

How could I explain to him that what scares me most is not dying but almost dying. I did not mind the idea of dying; how could I? Love and death are life's great desserts, aren't they? Isn't that what my limited experience of the human emotions had taught me?

"I've killed lots of men," Hector said. "Some faggots, too."

Do we bleed any differently, or is it just our blood that was under suspicion, I wondered.

"You won't be the first man I kill," Hector continued.

"Who was the first?" I asked.

He didn't hit me. Instead, he drove with less rodeo. "The man who killed my mother," he said, his voice sad with memory.

"Your mother was killed?"

"Yes, faggot, my mother was killed. All our mothers are killed."

I didn't quite understand. "Where?" I whispered.

And then Hector told the story of a New Year's Eve several years after his family moved to Miami from Puerto Rico. On New Year's Eve it is apparently a tradition to shoot gunfire into the sky at midnight; there are deaths by default. "My mother did everything to protect us; I was eleven years old. She made us stay indoors. 'Close the front door; get away from the windows,' she said. But right after midnight these shots like a war. Do you know what that is? Bullets, man, thousands of bullets, and one came right through the window and through a lamp shade and it hit my mother in her heart and she was dead."

Hector's mother, he said, had died in his father's arms. Hector took to the streets with his father's gun and asked questions and determined who shot the gun that killed his mother, and when Hector found him, he killed him. "A Cuban, some fucking Cuban faggot," Hector said. "The fucking police, man, what the fuck? Every year they tell people not to fire their guns in the air because everything that goes up must come down, but every New Year more killings."

"Time in jail?" I asked.

"I always kill in self-defense," Hector answered and stared at me.

Finally, I thought, we might be getting somewhere. Maybe, even, this whole unfortunate day would end with a laugh and a giggle and we'd all meet for sushi happily ever after once a year. But such are the follies of an optimist. "What is your name?" I asked Hector's daughter.

"Shut the fuck up, faggot! Think how you want to die!" Hector screamed, the words curling on his lips; he spit.

I closed my eyes, the motion of the car tumbled in my stomach, and I waited.

FOURTEEN

...

Is it any surprise that I was one of those children, one of those little boys, who could not throw a ball or catch one, well, unless it was huge, inflatable, with double summer colors?

Nonetheless, I owned two baseballs and two mitts, for hardball and softball. Baseball, and an affinity for the Boston Red Sox, was an essential component of any New England life. So one especially silent August afternoon that summer in 1962 when I was eight years old I stood alone in what was officially my bedroom and held my softball like a heart of twine in my hands.

It was a perfectly still Sunday afternoon. The plain room on the ground floor of our house had two windows; the view was of my father's garden, the weeping willow tree, and, in the distance, our neighbor's kitchen door, which one could see, or not, depending on which way the breeze, if any, blew the leaves of the tree.

Something compelled me to wonder what would happen if I threw the softball through the window. I tried not to but hurled the orb through the glass. I expected stars and icicles; instead, I was startled by the noise I had made, this thunder, and then the longest silence, which cried out; I waited.

The window glass was shattered; there wasn't any wind. Otherwise, nothing happened, absolutely nothing. I felt afraid and also exhilarated. My grandmother, who rarely left her apartment upstairs in the days and weeks until she joined my grandfather at the old-age home, walked past the window and looked in. Her white hair was like snow out of season; she smiled and handed me the softball through the broken window glass.

Nothing else happened. Later, I was punished by my father, who spoke to me in hoarse tones about the expense of repairing the broken glass. "Bad boy, Jules, bad boy," he said, his hand raised, then withdrawn, lest he hit me; did I detect a twinkle of pride in his eyes?

Otherwise, and like most days, the anthem of loneliness continued, silent and unabated, a favorite family song.

But if that summer at the ripe old age of eight I still had not mastered the fine boyhood arts of tying one's shoes or playing baseball, I somehow learned to ride a bicycle. The next morning my father got me up and dressed; I had been pretending, with a pillow clutched to my stomach, that I was pregnant. In our neighborhood the women were always having babies; across the street, at my friend Arthur's house, his mother was expecting her eighth child. Arthur told us about a trail of blood left in his front hall when his mother had her seventh child.

My mother was drinking coffee and smoking a cigarette in the kitchen. My father offered me breakfast, some cereal and juice. "I'll take Jules for his haircut," he told my mother.

"Fine; good idea," she said. The telephone rang, and she answered; it was Aunt Libby on the line.

I took my father's hand, and we walked to town, past a large Victorian house that was converted to apartments; my mother did not care for the people who lived there. Behind the house was some wooded, vacant land the children in the neighborhood considered a forest. My father was silent; we walked.

We stopped at his Pontiac garage; there was the smell of grease and the rattle of commerce. My mother said the salesmen wore suits that were too shiny if any good was ever to come to these men. The mechanics wore white T-shirts gone brown with sweat and oil; it was a warm day. The men fussed over me; I was their boss's son after all. I was tickled, bounced, and one man took me on his back and raced across the car lot like a wild animal; I held on to his shirt and the hair on the back of his neck. The big thrill was watching the hydraulic lift work; it raised a gray and white Pontiac coupe and I got to walk underneath it.

"Jules is getting a haircut today," my father explained.

The men exclaimed and laughed. My father took my hand, and we crossed the street to the barber shop; the man behind the cash register gave us a grand greeting, although he mistook me for my father's grandson. When something hurt my father, dark circles flooded underneath his eyes; I liked the mistake even less. I was lifted into the barber's chair and covered with a starched white apron. "A shave, or just a haircut?" the barber asked, his hands squeezing my shoulders.

Scissors clipped in time with a popular song playing on the radio; my hair, wet with tap water, dripped on the white apron.

"Your boy?" the man in the next chair inquired of my father.

My father smiled politely. He nodded his head.

The man who had spoken to my father was very tan. His face was covered in a beard of shaving cream. He had, or at least I thought he had, dark purple eyes; an attendant polished his black, wing-tip shoes until they shined like marble. "I have three sons," the man said, before the barber slid a razor over his beard.

His barber and mine exchanged curious looks. You could tell they distrusted this man.

"Three fine boys," the man continued as the barber's razor ran toward his lips.

The man watched me in the mirror. I felt like soup in the chair. Scissors sang in my hair; a proper part was arranged on the left side of my head. A scented shellac was applied; my hair was crisp as brown eggshell. The apron was removed, and I spilled to the floor. My father rested his hands on my shoulders, paid the bill, and asked if I wouldn't like a Coca-Cola at the drugstore fountain. The Liggett's was next door to my father's Pontiac garage; inside there was a commotion of people, parents and children, who came for the drawing of a raffle prize.

"I bought you a few tickets last week," my father explained.

I sat on a red leatherette stool and sipped Coca-Cola; I heard my name called. I'd won a Schwinn bicycle. No one cheered.

We walked the bicycle home. In front of one of the Victorian houses I noticed a sign I'd never seen before; "Goldenrod," it read, "incorporated 1629. The rose of New England."

"Something for nothing," my mother said, smiled, and kissed me on the forehead when we returned.

My best friend, Michael, sensing something special, I suppose, knocked on the kitchen door. I showed him the bike; he said he would teach me how to ride it. We pushed the bicycle to the end of the driveway, and Michael showed me how to get on, how to stay on, how to pedal and brake. I got on, and fell off. I got on again, and fell off again. He held the seat of the bike as I pedaled. He pushed me down Terry Avenue and let go; I fell again. We didn't give up; finally, after our umpteenth try, he let go and I wobbled alone but did not fall. Rotation by rotation, I found my seating on the contraption; then I was off. Eureka! I was off riding a bike, past the neighbors, past Dana Deamour, who was lying upside down on a chair reading a book on her porch; her blond ponytail swept the gray wood porch.

Emboldened, I picked up speed. I turned the corner and rounded the bend; I reversed my path and rode east, faster and faster, down Kinney Avenue and onto Main Street with its bigger curves and houses. Only when the speed of myself on the road knotted in my stomach did I have the thought I need never go home; I hit a tree, flew over the handlebars, and landed like a sponge of blood. I looked up; it was the same elm tree Dana Deamour had collided with in the hurricane. Goldenrod, after all, was a small town.

Bloodied, my head down, I walked the bike home. Michael had been chasing me; we laughed. "It's okay," he said.

Was it? My appearance upset my mother. "Jules! Blood!" she said.

Michael watched as my mother cleaned my wounds and wrapped me in bandages.

"You know," my father said, coming in from his garden still holding his wood-handled cutting shears in his hand, "school starts next week. And you're old enough for Hebrew school, too," he added.

"But Saul," my mother said, rinsing her hands of my blood in the kitchen sink.

"Jules has to go to Hebrew school, Leah," my father said.

Michael went home. My mother started dinner; my father poured highballs. I ate a few bites of chicken and went to bed early. On my parents' bed my mother kept a doll dressed in a bridal gown; at bedtime the doll was rested on the ash wood bureau. I took the doll to bed and drifted to sleep, all the while feeling the speed and the wind of my bike ride.

Our eighth summer ended.

FIFTEEN

...

I haven't mentioned the potholes. The potholes! The whirling, and the twirling, that morning on the highways around New York! Another crater and wham! Hit and never miss! We'd elevate like fools in a sleigh over our universe and land with a thump and a parched skid, each near crash promising the McCaulay's Driving School Dodge's last gasp.

"Faggot," Hector spit.

Never once were his hands ten-to-two on the steering wheel, as all good learning-to-drive manuals instruct us. We'd run out of air; I couldn't breathe. "Please open your window," I begged Hector. Stupid me; he slammed his fist against my ribs.

"Open the window? For the pussy boy wonder?"

I counted Yield signs; I bled sweat in my seat. Another pothole! Whee, wow! I closed my eyes; I remembered.

SIXTEEN

...

I went back to school; Jackie Kennedy redecorated the White House. On Sundays, we studied the state of Israel at Hebrew school. In the winter, I was told that my grandfather had died; my grandmother, who moved to the home for the aged just a few months before, died that spring. Far enough removed from the concerns of my elders, I never saw it happen; their deaths were not discussed.

But summer came again; I could rest my head again on a pillow of long days at home. Or could I? Aunt Joan, my father's sister-in-law, had long felt my only-child status was unnatural. Her solution? Anything that would socialize me into the fraternal habits of other children. That summer, she said, Enchanted Woods, a camp about an hour away near Hadlyme, was the answer.

"Where are we going?" I asked the morning I saw my mother packing a suitcase for me.

"To Enchanted Woods, Jules," my father answered, toying with the keys to a new Pontiac.

There was no point in objecting. My mother kissed me goodbye; I followed my father to the car.

We drove. Arriving at the camp, I saw log cabins and wooden shacks, a dark lake, a congestion of trees, and a lingering waterless sky. My father parked the Pontiac by a sign in the campground that read, "New Friends," and we walked to a hut with the sign "Welcome Boys."

My father rang the metal bell on the desk; there were framed maps of the wilderness on the wall. A bright-eyed man, blond, wearing a T-shirt with the Enchanted Woods logo, alighted in the cabin. He was someone Dana Deamour might like, I thought.

"Hi! My name's Tom," he said, "and this, Mr. Orr, must be your grandson, Jules."

"My son," my father said.

"Of course, sir, your son," Tom said. "Well, come on, Jules, the candy shop is open every afternoon after sports, and it is open now. We'd better hurry; you like candy, don't you?"

Candy and roses, yes, I thought.

An unseasonable gust of cool air seemed to blow my father to his Pontiac. Tom settled his large, tanned hand on the back of my neck; he turned my head away from too long a view of my father's departure. My stomach fell; it would have choked me at my ankles had Tom not been so chatty, so insistent that we get to the candy shop before closing.

Tom kept his hand on the back of my neck for nearly the rest of the day. Sometimes he would remove it to rake through his blond hair, but the hand was back to guide me through unpacking and changing into shorts and an Enchanted Woods T-shirt in time for dinner. Tom explained that everything would be all right although, he said, the other campers had arrived the week before. Already they were a community excelling in sports, crafts, ghost stories, and the swallowing of burned marshmallows. I felt like the postscript to their jolly season.

But there was Tom, his hand always at the back of my neck.

Before bed we were meant to take showers. I'd never taken a shower and was reluctant. I was used only to baths in Goldenrod; sometimes my mother still soaped my head with fragrant soaps she ordered from the department store in Hartford. Tom told me to remove my clothes; he did the same. We left them on a wood bench near the shower room. We showered together; everywhere I looked Tom was a big man.

After showering, the other boys sang by the campfire outside our cabin. Then we got into infirmary beds; it was time for lights out. Only for a few minutes were they quiet; then the other boys began to whisper, to giggle. Tom, whose bed was in a single room that adjoined ours, yelled for everyone to quiet down. "Hush up, boys," he called. "I want no repeat of last night—got that? That means you, Harold, you too, Sidney . . . Carl, cut it out. Go to sleep; you need rest before tomorrow's swimming championships."

Swimming championships? Couldn't we ride bikes instead? Most of the other boys had fallen asleep; a few gossiped, one or two seemed to be switching cots. You would hear footsteps; maybe there were animals inside the cabin! Tom returned. "Quiet down, and I mean it this time," he said, his voice nearly unfriendly.

"Jules, you all right?" Tom asked. He was standing over my cot.

"Yes, sure, uh, I mean no; I don't know," I stammered.

"The first night away from home is tough," he said, sitting down at the edge of the bed.

"Tommy's boy," one of the others whistled.

"Go to sleep, all of you," Tom yelled, his hand resting on my leg. Moonlight creeped through the window like hot wax. Tom left me alone.

I could not sleep; every sound startled me until I was more awake than I'd ever been at such a late hour. I had this awful feeling of having no place, no place to stay, no place to go. I figured if I listened to the wind long enough, morning would come. Then it rained, at first a light tapping on the roof of the cabin, then thunder, then the downpour. Enchanted Woods was drowning, and still it was indescribably hot.

"Jules, you aren't asleep." It was Tom again.

He sat on the side of my bed. He brushed my head with his hand. "It's your first night; you can sleep with me," he said.

I followed him to his cot in the other room. He pulled open his covers, and I lay down next to him on a rumpled white sheet. "It's so damn hot," he said and removed his pajamas. I rolled into his body; unlike my father he had almost no hair anywhere. The thunder, and the rain, sounded like cats slugged across the black sky. Tom, asleep, snored.

He rolled a lot in the night; I fell under him. He never was still; he mentioned the name Anne often and sweated; he moved like I might when riding my bike uphill. I couldn't breathe; Tom was a very big man. Some of his sweat exploded on my stomach and dried white. I couldn't yell; I wasn't Anne.

In the morning, we all jumped—some more enthusiastically than others—into the lake before breakfast.

I guess I had slept; I couldn't remember when it stopped raining nor when the sun rose. Tom said I needn't worry about the swimming championship; I could watch. Throughout the championship, as boys raced in the lake and hooted and whistled, I could only watch Tom. Someone would say something to me, or tell me where to go or what to do next, and I would look toward Tom to see what he thought. Might it rain again tonight?

That afternoon, the campers and the instructors assembled in front of the activities hut for what was promised as a special treat.

It was a guest speaker, a tall man who wore a safari suit. He talked about his adventures in the jungle; he entertained us with animals he let out of cages act by act: a raccoon, a squirrel, a falcon. If you raised your hand high enough, you might get to go up front and pet the animals.

"Now I need a very special volunteer, a courageous boy," said the animal trainer in the safari suit.

Whatever it was, I knew this was a chance to distinguish myself. I caught Tom's eye; he nodded.

The animal trainer chose me. "Close your eyes for a big surprise," he whispered.

I faced my comrade campers; I closed my eyes. I heard gasps; the trainer told me to keep my eyes shut and remain very still. He wrapped something indescribably muscular, cold, and as wet as it was dry around my neck. I felt exhilarated by the open-mouthed awe I sensed from the other campers. For a second I thought it was Tom's arm at my neck; I was wrong. Whatever was wrapped around me constricted; I opened my eyes and saw the snake. Its agate night eyes slid at mine; I could no longer breathe. The snake convulsed; its head turned downward and slid toward my stomach and thighs. I looked for Tom's eyes.

What happened next?

"Come on, Jules, I'll take you home," my father said. I opened my eyes; he was standing over my cot in the camp's infirmary.

I started to cry.

"Just don't cry," he said, "for Christ's sake don't cry."

Tom was there; he carried my suitcase. "The swimming championships were exceptionally fine yesterday, Mr. Orr. We're sorry Jules missed the last session yesterday afternoon. Are you sure he wants to go home? We start canoeing lessons tomorrow," Tom said. He wore a red bathing suit, white sneakers, no socks or shirt.

"I think Jules should come home with me, yes," my father said.

Tom looked at me; he brushed my hair off my forehead.

"Don't you find it rather chilly without a shirt?" my father asked the camp counselor.

Tom removed his hand from my hair. "Jules is very restless in his sleep," he laughed.

"Is he?" my father replied, looking from Tom to me and back again. "Then he really had better come home with me."

My father put his hand on the back of my neck and led me to his car.

SEVENTEEN

...

Why don't we just call it a day and go home?" I begged Hector.

"You're home, faggot," Hector responded, slamming his fist into my gut.

"You're with me."

EIGHTEEN

. . .

Michael rushed to greet me almost the moment we drove up the drive in Goldenrod. The outing to Enchanted Woods was over.

"So how was it?" Michael asked.

"Oh, you know."

"Yeah, a bunch of stuck-ups; my mother thought so."

"Yeah," I said, "stuck-ups. Let's ride bikes."

We spent our summer days on our bikes; Michael had discovered a dirt path in the woods that led down to the banks of the Thames River, named for the original; its delta was in New London. We rode our bikes to the river after lunch and rolled in the dirt and searched for frogs and salamanders until it felt like it was time to go home. Michael and I? We didn't talk much; we had the fascinations of wet earth and blue sky and the promise of bugs and flies. And Michael always cast a shadow of safety over us.

One morning, a few days back from my brief experiment in outdoor living at Enchanted Woods, I woke up and felt ill. What could the matter be?

My father wasn't next to me. I got dressed and went to the kitchen. He wasn't there; I looked through the screen door to his garden and didn't see him. My mother was pinching the fingers of her white gloves to fit her hands. She wore a blue linen dress with a black patent leather belt; she smiled. "I thought I might walk into town for a little shopping, darling, it's such a beautiful day," she said. "Wouldn't you like to come with me? We don't do much together, and we should."

I remember gazing into her eyes and falling into her smile. "Where's Daddy?" I asked.

"He got up early; he said he couldn't sleep," answered my mother. She lighted a cigarette. "He seems to be terribly worried about the ash trees out front; he's been tending to them for nearly an hour now. All right, stay here then and keep your father company; give him a kiss from me, Jules, and tell him I won't be long in town."

My mother walked to the kitchen screen door; I watched her with some kind of new interest. "What is it, darling?" she asked, aware of this sudden intensity from me. "Is there something special you want me to buy you?"

"No, Mommy," I answered.

She walked toward me from the door and bent over. She scooped my chin in her gloved hand and kissed me on my forehead for what seemed the most delightful, if inexplicably long, time. "I'm so glad you decided to get yourself out of Enchanted Woods. I didn't want you to go in the first place; it was your father's idea, and he was miserable without his favorite playmate."

The screen door closed behind her; I watched from the kitchen table as she evaporated toward town. I got myself some cereal; I watched three summertime flies fight to get inside. I remembered my father, whom my mother said I would find at the front of the house. This was not my route or normal place; we came and went from the rear of the house almost always, where the kitchen and driveway to Terry Avenue were. To get to the front of the house meant walking through the formal rooms, the dining room and parlor, all still lifes of imposing, solitary furniture and landscape paintings in ornate gilded frames on the walls. Our house could be explained in four chambers: the familiar back with the kitchen and our bedrooms, the front quarters with the more stately rooms, the forbidding entry hall where strangers called, and the sweeping white stairway that led to what had been my grandparents' place, similarly divided, upstairs.

I opened the heavy, mahogany front door and at the corner of the porch looking right found my father rocking in a white wicker chair. He was singing, I thought, except it seemed a particularly dark song, a ditty from a nightmare. My father's shirt was unbuttoned; he slouched in the rocking chair. His hands clutched at his chest, as if he had caught us a cardinal, a bright red pet.

I felt ill; what could the matter be? Just to walk, I had to imagine I was pedaling up a hill.

A terror had convulsed my father's face. His breath came in short, hydraulic gasps. "Jules," he managed to say, "Jules . . ."

"What is it? What's wrong?"

My father opened his hands; no cardinal rose.

"Daddy?"

"Help . . ."

I rushed to Michael's house; I yelled through his kitchen door. Michael's father, the football coach at the local high school, followed by Mrs. Grosvenor, ran to help my father.

From east and west, the neighbors watched a red ambulance capture my father. Michael's father rode with my father to the hospital; he held the oxygen mask to his face. Michael's mother drove into town to find my mother. Michael and I sat on the front steps of our house. We didn't talk. We heard the echo of the ambulance sirens instead.

I loved my father; then he died.

Actually, it was a matter of a few weeks, and a house filled with relations tending to my mother and me, before my father died. We lived on tenterhooks and nibbling affections; we waited. Our house was possessed by dreadful expectations. Children under the age of twelve were not allowed to visit the hospital, but on my birthday, in the middle of July, my father telephoned from the hospital. His nurse had dialed the phone and held the receiver to his mouth.

"Jules." I could barely hear him.

"Daddy!"

He began to cry; the nurse fumbled nervously to get him off the phone. "Your father wanted to wish you a happy birthday, Jim," she said.

I could hear my father crying; the phone receiver crashed like glass in its cradle. I listened nonetheless until one of my relations told me to hang up; I was tying up the line. I watched the phone nonstop, expecting him to call back; I tried to be the one who answered it every time. Two mornings later when the phone rang, I answered. A man's voice I did not recognize asked to speak with my mother. Their conversation was brief. She slid the receiver from the palm of her hand and sighed.

"Well, Jules, it's over."

What is over, I wanted to know. Summer? The baseball season? Polio? The World? But I knew what she meant; cars no longer needed to crash on Main Street for me to understand.

I knew.

Doors and windows closed. Mirrors were draped in black cloth. The confirmation of my father's death shook the house like a bedspread beaten on a clothesline; we all wore black. Whatever inner exultations might have made my mother jaunty before left her now. The rest of her life, about ten years, she made do with windless sails.

Aunt Libby, wearing a black V-neck sweater and tunnel-tight skirt, awakened my mother on the morning of my father's funeral. It was decided by a jury of my relations that I was too young to attend the ceremony and burial. Instead, a cousin named Kate, who was the gamine, Audrey Hepburn type in our clan, was appointed my caretaker. As a line of black cars snaked up our driveway before the service, Kate fetched me in her family's Pontiac and drove me to her house on the other side of Goldenrod. I could eat all the brownies I wanted to that day, she said; I could play with her dolls and stuffed animals. Kate was an undergraduate student at the University of Boston home on summer break; she talked most of the morning on the telephone while I played.

Around lunchtime her beau, Phillip, arrived jolly as a television clown. Phillip had just graduated that spring from Harvard; he was going to travel in Europe for a year, and that made Kate miserable. He already had a foreign car, an MG sports coupe; we went for a ride the day my father was buried. Phillip had black hair thick as a cat's; he wore baggy khaki trousers, a white T-shirt, and tennis shoes. Kate wore a sleeveless black dress, a strand of pearls, and Norell perfume, a smoky floral scent. I sat next to my cousin in the bucket seat while she flirted over my head with Phillip. Whenever he shifted gears, the stick shift collided with my thigh.

We went all over town in Phillip's speedy convertible sports car. We had a picnic in the town's park; when I remembered my father, my stomach sank to my knees. But Phillip told jokes, and I just laughed and laughed; it was the most wonderful day, I thought, but we had to go home.

Terry Avenue and our driveway were dammed with cars. There were mourners on the porch, mourners in the house, mourners on the lawn. Kate gave me her hand, and, like a Roman princess, she walked perfectly erect through the crowds. Phillip kept his hand on my head; we looked for my mother. Women in black clothes had taken over our kitchen. Men in black sat shiva in the living room, wailing the Hebrew Yahrzeit over and over. Kaddish. The Jewish Muzak.

I sat at the kitchen table, in the chair where my mother had left her black widow's veil. How many sweet cakes could the women around the table get me to eat? I ate. The women gossiped, then, remembering I was there, would say something they thought would be appeasing. "Oh, Jules, if you only knew how happy your father was the day you were born, and born a boy yet," a relation said and handed me a plate of warm raisin kugel and dry brownies.

"That ring Saul gave Leah when Jules was born?" exclaimed another lady. "Have you ever, did you know they had sapphires so big?"

The kitchen chorus sang that they most certainly hadn't.

Phillip explained how he wished he could stay to say Kaddish, but he had to go; his parents were expecting him at home. He might try to stop back. "Keep it up, sport," he told me and left.

"Nice fella," the women cooed when the screen door closed.

Kate blushed. She giggled with the ladies about her Phillip; she was hungry, she had some kugel.

"So did Jules cry a lot? He always cries a lot," I heard Aunt Joan ask her daughter, Kate.

"Not once," Kate whispered, shaking her head.

Aunt Libby said my mother was resting in my father's room, but she would wake her.

I waited to see my mother; she was a long time coming. I felt uncomfortable with the women; I was confused by their sociability. I couldn't wait for my mother any longer. I grabbed her veil off the back of the kitchen chair and put it over my head; I ran out of the kitchen and down the drive toward Dana Deamour's house on Terry Avenue. The veil, lush with fluidity, seemed like something with wings on a Saturday morning cartoon.

Dana's house was dark. Mrs. Stanley and Dana's mother, Esther, were still at our house, but I hoped I might find Dana. It was coming on sunset when I entered her house. The kitchen was dark, the living room gray. You could barely make out a copy of a painting on the wall that I had always liked; it showed three people tumbling in a wave.

Mrs. Stanley, besides cleaning for my mother, earned extra money working as a seamstress; I saw the flickering of candlelight from her sewing room, which was in the back of the house.

The door was open; I walked in.

On the sofa, on top of the neighbors' clothes left for mending, Dana lay, her hair not tied in a ponytail. On top of Dana was a man; he was naked down to the khaki trousers wrapped around his ankles. His buttocks were clenched like two baseball mitts sweating the seventh inning; the muscles in his legs rippled like a bicycle racer's at a downhill turn. This strong man was very tan; even in the shadows his buttocks burned white from the box shape of a bathing suit.

The couple's shadow, in candlelight, jittered on the ceiling of the sewing room. Dana's legs swallowed the tan man at his waist; her face was buried in the mending. Her fingers plowed the man's thick, black hair. He seemed to ride so deep he might fall through.

I watched.

I did not move.

They made these sounds. Dana's legs tightened like a wishbone around her visitor's waist. The sofa banged against the wall; he swallowed words: "Oh, baby, baby."

I knew I had to leave without being noticed; I tripped on my mother's veil.

Dana shot up like sparks.

The man fell aside.

His cock.

"Jules," Dana hissed.

"Shit," the man spit.

"What are you doing?" Dana yelled. "How long have you been standing there?"

I did not answer.

I ran and ran, even when Phillip hollered my name.

Looking from the road to my house, I saw that the mourners were still there; I sat across the street in an empty lot and watched our home flicker with Kaddish and company.

Was I missed? The sun had set. The sky was ripped with stripes of ambulance red. From the distance, a woman danced toward me. I heard her sing some kind of song about washing a man from her hair. "Hello there, dearie," the woman said and plopped herself in front of me on the grass.

I recognized Mrs. Warner from the other side of the neighborhood. My mother did not approve of her; she said Dana Deamour would end up like Mrs. Warner if she wasn't careful.

Mrs. Warner was distinguished by a mop of curly hair; most of it dangled where her bobbypins had given out. She wore rows of fake pearls and jet black beads, a black slip, and no brassiere. A sequin bag dangled from a tarnished silver chain over her shoulder; she was barefoot and woozy. I recognized the smell of rye whiskey; it was one of the ingredients for my father's highballs. "Pattycake, pattycake, baker's man," she sang and tried to ply this children's game against my palms.

I raised my hands; Mrs. Warner kept missing.

Her eyes were purple; maybe they were blue before sunset. Three rings of red lipstick circled her mouth; some of it rested on her lips, most of it smudged her teeth. I noticed that the soles of her feet were black with mud. "Made for dancing," she laughed, raising a foot toward my head. Mrs. Warner wasn't wearing underpants.

"My father died," I said.

"I know, you poor son of a bitch," she shook her head. "Nice man, your father. The only bastard in this goddamn town who ever gave me the time of day when times got tough. A real gentleman."

I didn't understand what she meant.

"I'm the town drunk; every town has one, sweetheart. Slip, and lust will make you crazy," she said, unscrewing the top of a leather and silver flask. She drank.

"Try it?" Mrs. Warner handed me the flask. "Swallow, don't think," she instructed.

As the liquor snaked its way into my gut, it burned; I must have grimaced.

"Now, don't puke, kid, for Christ's sake don't go puking up my hard-earned booze, baby," she warned me. "I ain't made of money, not like them fancy phonies of yours inside."

With all the lights on and silhouettes of people against the windows, our house burned like a birthday cake in the otherwise dark, sober neighborhood. "I was nine years old last week," I told Mrs. Warner and took another swig of rye whiskey.

"Happy fucking birthday, baby," she laughed. "Speaking of which . . . who is the joe Dana Deamour is fucking tonight? You know his name?"

"Excuse me, Mrs. Warner?" I said, astonished.

"Ah, forget it, kid; I seen you sneaking into that house. I seen you watching them go at it," she said. "His cock? Some fine cock, a real king dolphin; I wouldn't say no to slamming that piece right home here in ye old chapel of love." She rubbed her hand under her belly.

Mrs. Warner took another gulp of whiskey and handed me the flask. "That's what we all want, baby, the cock of God, and I am talking to you specifically, particularly, physically, and theologically, baby." She leaned forward and rubbed her face in my stomach. "Problem with people is they don't know it; send 'em up flying in the highest, mightiest airplanes for a closer look, even, and they don't get it. We're all wanting for the cock of God." She raised her head stately then and stood up.

Mrs. Warner crossed the street and wandered toward my father's rose bushes. She plucked the flowers from their stems, breaking the buds with her hands. "My old man's gone now. Gone cold as Alaska now. Can't explain," she sort of sang. "Dance with me, little boy, I'm all yours, all yours, at the new, reduced rate of eight cents a dance." Mrs. Warner pricked herself on a thorn. The sight of blood upset her; she wrapped her finger in my mother's black veil and fell silent. The neighborhood tilted, the whiskey in me, I supposed; Mrs. Warner ran off but left the veil with me.

"Did you go see Dana?" Mrs. Stanley asked when I came through the kitchen door.

"No, ma'am," I answered.

I carried my mother's veil to my father's room, where I would sleep, and opened the door. Aunt Libby was sitting on the bed; I could tell I had interrupted something, a conversation. My mother stood in front of the bureau putting lipstick on—she saw me in the mirror. She wore a black slip and pearls. She put the lipstick down on a silver tray and draped the black cloth over the mirror again. She turned to me; she clutched her bridal doll in her arms and didn't speak. She swayed against the bureau and shook her head. She was crying.

Aunt Libby took me by the hand and led me from the room. "Why don't you lie down, too," my aunt said.

"Is Mommy all right?" I asked.

"Oh, well, she will be in time; we all will," Aunt Libby answered.

"Everything's changed," I said.

"Everything is changed, Jules, but it's strange: the older I get, I find the more things change, the more they stay the same."

I didn't understand; Aunt Libby returned to my mother.

I still had the black veil; I lay down with it on the bed that was officially mine but in which I never had slept. A while later, my mother entered the room. She was dressed; she wore black, of course, a blouse and a skirt. "I have to say good night to everyone; I almost forgot my guests," my mother said softly. "Jules," she continued, "if you don't mind, I think it is best if you sleep in this room from now on. I had Mrs. Graves change the linen for you this afternoon."

Mrs. Graves was the lady who helped Mrs. Stanley when there were parties at our house. No sooner was her name mentioned than she appeared. "Comfy, son?" she asked. Against the black of mourning she offered considerable contrast; Mrs. Graves wore blue denim pedal pushers, a red gingham shirt, yellow flipflops, and a green headband around her white hair. "Here are your towels," she said; I felt like a houseguest might.

My mother sighed. She unbuttoned her blouse at the neck; she fingered her pearls. "I'm so tired, so thoroughly exhausted. I wish everyone would just go home."

She closed the door to my room; I squeezed her veil. The room was very plain and quiet; you could hear the mourners in the distance.

"Pssst," a voice whispered at the window.

It was Dana Deamour. "What are you doing?" she asked, her face pressed against the mosquito screen.

"My father died."

"I know." A silence. "My hair is wet," Dana said.

"Is it?" I asked.

"I just washed it. Come on, come with me."

"Where? I can't, I'll get into trouble."

"You'll never get into trouble around here again," she said.

"What do you mean?" I asked.

"My grandmother says now that your father's gone up, there's no one here who would dare lay a hand on you even if you needed it."

"My mother is here," I said. "She is saying good night to everyone now."

"My grandmother says your mother is scared of you."

"Why?"

"Just come on, Jules; I brought a box for you to climb down on. Come out through the window, and let's go!"

"Where?"

"Just hurry. My hair is wet. It has to dry fast."

I raised the mosquito screen; I climbed over the sill and onto the box Dana had waiting for me on the ground. "Good," she said, leaning forward; I thought she might kiss me. I thought about having seen her with Phillip just an hour or two before; I wondered if she was going to say anything. Should I?

Dana took my hand, and we ran toward the end of the driveway; her blond hair rippled with the moonlight. She stopped; she looked me in the eyes: "Did you tell anyone?"

"No."

"Are you going to tell anyone?"

"Never."

"Good, then you keep the box."

"Why?"

"For great escapes," she laughed. "I'll come see you tomorrow," she promised and ran home.

The mourners were beginning to go home; I hid behind the rose bushes so as not to be seen. Back at my window, I mounted the box and was about to climb inside when I saw the bedroom door open. It was Phillip, who had changed his clothes and now wore a jacket and tie; I hadn't seen him return to our house. He shrugged; he closed the door. I climbed through the window and lowered the screen. I undressed quickly; I got into bed and turned the lights out. Before I fell asleep, the bedroom door opened. From the light in the hall, I saw my mother.

She held her wedding doll. Even if Phillip had told her he hadn't found me, she never asked where I had been.

NINETEEN

· · ·

The McCaulay's Driving School Dodge, with Hector at the wheel, nearly consumed a well-mannered blue Volvo station wagon in the lane next to us. Hector hit the brakes, then sped on.

"Please, Hector," I pleaded. "This is all a terrible misunderstanding. Pull over to the side of the road and let's talk. We can work this out."

"Shut up, asshole."

"We're grown men; we can talk this out!"

"Papa!" Hector's daughter screamed when we almost collided with a truck.

"Anything can be solved with honest communication," I said.

Hector slapped my head with the palm of his hand. He lighted a cigarette.

"Shut up! Shut up. It's never enough for you, is it, faggot? Nothing is ever enough," he exhaled.

TWENTY

...

The next morning, after my father was buried, I woke up and remembered he was dead; the news fell like a stone on a grave. That is what it was like: I would forget and remember. Thirty years later it is still very much the same way. He is gone and out of mind; something happens, something someone says, or something I see, and he is reconstituted as thoroughly as the whims of memory will allow.

I looked out the window of my bedroom. The box Dana Deamour had left was still there; I remembered he was dead. I forgot he was dead when, in the kitchen, I saw Dana's mother, Esther, and Mrs. Stanley eating cinnamon buns; I was hungry, too. Then I remembered my father was dead. And it wasn't just sadness, or fear, I felt but this heavy weight that pushed me away from the center of the world as I had known it, like I was being swept against the sides of an ice rink, I imagined. When Mrs. Stanley wondered when it would rain, said Goldenrod needed rain for its roses, I remembered that my father was dead.

I rested my cinnamon bun on a plate; I watched the first of the men, the black mourners, arrive to sit shiva in the living room, which they would do for a week, divining the Kaddish, their wail interrupted only for sweet rolls and coffee. Aunt Libby came up the path; she wore another black sweater and skirt. She carried summer flowers for my mother.

"Libby?"

"Leah," my aunt answered when my mother first appeared. She took the flowers from her sister, tried to smile, and put them in a clear vase with water. Thinking of something else, my mother left the vase near the sink and walked outdoors onto the porch. She stood there, alone, thinking about what I do not know. She stared out the driveway; she fingered the pearls at her neck.

"I could move, couldn't I," she said to no one in particular.

Aunt Libby opened the screen door and stood next to her. "You've got the money; it might be a good thing."

I joined them on the porch; it was a warm day, but you might slip and freeze in the sun. I heard the men saying Kaddish; I studied my mother. The sun brushed her profile with white gold; her cheeks were slightly rouged, her face whisked with fresh pink powder. Her marble nose turned up; her eyes were pond green. She had a large bosom, a French tailored waist, impeccable posture, out-of-town shoes.

"I'm so tired," she sighed.

"Leah, eat," Aunt Libby said, taking her arm and leading her back inside the kitchen. "You've got to eat, darling."

"Eat, eat, we'll say you ate anyway," Mrs. Stanley said, pretending she had a Jewish accent.

"Eat, Mrs. Orr," Mrs. Graves said, wearing the same picnic-colored outfit as yesterday, "I want to clean up."

"Say I ate anyway," my mother said.

The telephone rang; my mother discussed my father's head-stone with her caller.

"What would you like to do today, Jules?" Aunt Libby asked me.

"Go for a ride," I answered.

My mother inquired about the merits of granite compared to marble.

"Actually," Aunt Libby said, "your friend Jeannie's mother called yesterday and suggested you might like to go there today and play with Jeannie and Peter. Aren't they your friends from school?"

Jeannie was the pretty girl at school; Peter was her boy-friend. But why should I see them today? I hadn't seen them all summer. "Why can't I play with Michael?"

"Because you've been invited to play with Jeannie and Peter; it isn't polite to break a date at the last minute," Aunt Libby explained. "Perhaps you can see Michael tomorrow."

"If we move, what about Michael?" I yelled toward my mother.

She put her hand over the receiver. "Darling, I'm talking on the phone," she said and looked to her sister for reinforcement.

I gave up before I even started; I got my shoes and followed Aunt Libby to the car.

At Jeannie's house, her mother greeted me at the front door; Mrs. McAlister, a young woman, bent down, and my head was lost in cascades of her sunflower blond hair. "Poor dear," she said, "poor, poor darling. I thought you'd be happier playing here than at the country club; Jeannie and Peter can play there anytime."

Country club? Oh yes, no Jews. I learned all about it in Hebrew school.

At the back of their house, which I remember mostly as pink and green with a lot of strawberry ashtrays, I found Jeannie and

Peter playing Twister, a game in which one attempts to extend one's hands and feet upon a variety of entangled markings on a jolly, colorful plastic mat. Jeannie, her head covered by her shag of long yellow hair, was bent over Peter, a thick, white-blond boy big for his age, who was splayed on the gameboard. "Hello, Julian," Jeannie said, not very enthusiastically.

I stood over the Twister mat and watched the two children play.

"I guess it's your turn," Jeannie shrugged.

I moved my left foot forward and put my right hand down. It was then Peter's turn; his right arm tripped my left leg, and I fell. I lay on my back, looked up into the blue Yankee sky, and remembered my father died. Jeannie and Peter skipped off to the swing set.

"Lunch, children," Mrs. McAlister called from the terrace.

Jeannie ran ahead.

"My father is never going to die," Peter hissed as we walked toward the luncheon table.

"My father didn't die," I said.

"Did so."

"Did not."

"Did so," Peter insisted.

"Did not!"

"Boys, stop it," Jeannie's mother reprimanded. "Really, Peter, where are your manners? Poor Julian is less fortunate than you."

I shivered in the sunlight; pink lemonade was poured into a strawberry-motif, plastic glass. A white linen napkin, with strawberry embroidery, was placed on my lap. Luncheon consisted of crustless tunafish sandwiches on white bread and carrot sticks. The bread was damp with mayonnaise. Jeannie's mother did all the talking, a breathless accounting of summer sailing lessons and tennis matches.

Eventually, the back door to the house opened, and Aunt Libby was there, standing quite in contrast, in her mourning black, to the pastel place. "Ready to go, Jules?"

I got up and thanked my hostess.

"You come back and play anytime, poor darling," she said and extended her hand for me to shake. Jeannie and Peter rushed back to the Twister mat.

"Jeannie's mother wondered if Peter might have upset you," Aunt Libby said as we drove home.

I shrugged; I remembered my father had died.

"I would imagine it would bother your little friends that your father died; it would make them feel uncomfortable to think it could happen to them," Aunt Libby said.

It wouldn't, I thought; wasn't I the only Goldenrod child expelled by this distinction?

The driveway to our house was filled with cars, the kitchen thick with women worried about my mother. The songs of Kaddish spilled through all the rooms as the men prayed in the parlor. "We'll want to take the ash trees and the sundial," my mother told a stranger, a man named Mr. Shugrue, who wore a gray suit and a brown hat.

"Leah, look at this kugel Helen brought; eat, darling," one of the ladies called to my mother.

"I'm fine," my mother said and kept talking to the man in the gray suit; he stood next to her like a shadow. "And we will want to be settled by Thanksgiving; we'll probably go to Miami in the winter, so any extra work can be finished while we are away," she said.

I gathered we were moving.

I wondered where Michael was; I hadn't seen him in a while. I walked to his house and knocked on the kitchen door. His mother answered. "Where's Michael?" I asked.

"Oh, Jules, dear." Mrs. Grosvenor seemed nervous.

I remembered my father was dead; I dreaded whatever she would say.

"He is visiting his grandparents," she said.

"Why?"

"Why? Well." She seemed startled, but she was a nice woman; she would tell at least a part of the truth. "Well, Michael's dad and I just felt, what with everything going on at your house – and you being so busy looking after your mother – that it would be better if Michael, and his brother, stayed with their grandparents for a couple of weeks. You understand."

I did; wasn't it what Aunt Libby had said? I walked along the borders of our lawns, past my father's roses parched by the days of sun and no rain as well as Mrs. Warner's lurchings. On the other side of the property were the ash trees and sundial my father loved. I read the inscription on the sundial; I never had paid it much mind before.

"Come along with me," it read, "the best is yet to be."

I sat down and leaned against it. In the breeze, I heard the Kaddish sung; I waited.

TWENTY-ONE

...

It was popular in the late 1970s, especially among such industries of self-actualization as est and Lifespring, to say God was a large, black lady.

"God is a large, black lady," someone from some New Age think tank would say on some talk show, or in some magazine article, and you were meant to titter with amusement at this flying in the face of convention.

Hector drove us off the Belt Parkway; we rumbled into a neighborhood in Queens. There were narrow, two-way streets, pizza parlors, laundromats, redbrick, multifamily houses the color of matchtops; Hector ran through stop lights unstopped.

"Faggot, you bother me," he spit, fumbling with the radio dial when the reception went fuzzy.

We sped down roads; pedestrians jumped out of our way. In the distance was a large, black elderly lady slowly crossing the street. Unbridled, Hector sped toward her.

I hoped, I prayed she would get out of our way.

She wore the jauntiest of red hats, a turquoise car coat, a paisley dress; she carried two sacks of groceries.

"Be careful!"

"Fuck you, faggot," Hector hissed.

"You're going to hit her!"

"What the fuck is your problem, faggot—shut up!" Hector yelled and slammed his fist against my head.

Hector hit the brakes; on impact the large, black lady rose slow-motion and fairylike—she smiled this forgiving smile—from the street. The turquoise car coat spread across the window like wings; she tumbled on the hood of the driving school Dodge. Her head hit hardball hard; the windshield fractured into a spider-web of shattered glass.

Blood washed from her face. Blood bathed the car.

She clutched her grocery bags; a loaf of Wonder Bread lodged under her chin.

Her eyes—the look of someone saddened by a surprise—locked on us through the splintered glass.

Blood ran down her face; Hector's daughter screamed.

The woman's eyes froze on us.

Hector's lip was cut when his head hit the steering wheel. He spit out a mouthful of blood. He rubbed his eyes; his daughter covered hers. Hector spit more blood. He rang the car horn, hoping that might get the woman off the hood of the Dodge.

The lady's jaunty red hat, saturated in blood, soaked purple and dripped to the ground.

TWENTY-TWO

· · ·

Our house emptied of mourners at the end of the week, the first days of August.

With great haste, my mother and I moved to our new house; it was brick and wood, a refurbished farmhouse, in the country-side on the outskirts of the village. Mr. Shugrue, the man in the gray suit who had shadowed my mother in the kitchen the day after my father was buried, helped decorate the house. He and my mother drove all over Connecticut shopping: winged chairs, love seats, Tiffany lamps, porcelain figurines, old bird prints in buffed wood frames. There were modern appointments, as well: a dish-washer, for instance, a color television for the "family room" off the kitchen, which is where my mother was most often ensconced. We ate at home only once or twice a week, when Aunt Libby might call, or my mother's best friend, Iris, whom I called Aunt Iris. She owned the bookshop in town.

I was to attend a different school that fall; I do not remember saying goodbye to Michael or Dana Deamour. "Of course they will visit," my mother promised, but they didn't.

I suppose we had moved up in the world, by spending money and buying a new, bigger house; it certainly was a different world.

A few days before school began I went for a physical, and one mystery was explained. I had begun to have trouble seeing after my father died; I needed eyeglasses. They were prescribed, and heavy black frames were measured and bought. I hated them. Whenever I could, I would slide them off my nose, and whatever I wanted to see, or did not want to see, as the case might have been, was dulled.

From the activities of my mother decorating her new house, the shopping trips with Mr. Shugrue or with assorted relations, I, too, became interested in houses, but not ours necessarily. I sat in front of the new color television and drew plans in sketch pads for imaginary houses. I got the idea from the shelter magazines that piled high in the family room during my mother's campaign to fashion her new house. Parallel lines indicated windows; slashes for doors. I liked pools and moats; I was particularly fond of atriums and five-car garages. They were vain houses; I never drew them with people.

My mother decorated her bedroom mostly all in purple, bed, curtains, carpet. Her bridal doll was rested in a lavender wood chest with glass front doors.

My father's sundial was settled on a rolling knoll of back lawn near a pagoda my mother had built over the brook that ran along the borders of our property. Beyond the brook were fields and a forest; without Michael I was reluctant to explore there alone. Sometimes you would see deer on the lawn; when raccoons discovered our trash cans, my mother had a house built for the refuse, too. On the Sunday of the weekend before school began that year, Goldenrod celebrated its two hundredth anniversary with a grand parade. Some of the town's streets were actually covered with gold leaf; I still have a small, brown ceramic urn half filled with the golden chips my cousin Sarah and I collected that weekend.

My mother and I drove to my father's garage in town; folding chairs were set up on a flatbed truck so all the Orrs could watch the parade come down Main Street. My mother wore a new blue linen dress and a diamond heart necklace my father had given her. I'd never seen it; now she wore it all the time, these bright chips in a heart-shaped setting on a platinum chain.

All the relations, most of their friends, and the garage employees and their families were there: Uncle Israel and his new wife, Aunt Gladys; Aunt Joan and her daughters, Sarah and Kate; Kate's beau, Phillip; "Aunt Iris" and her son, Ben; Aunt Libby; Mrs. Stanley and her daughter, Esther. Dana Deamour was marching in the parade, twirling a baton, Mrs. Stanley boasted.

"I guess Jules will see the parade better than any of us with those nice new glasses of his," my cousin Charles said, sipping a Coca-Cola.

My mother had sold my father's Pontiac business to Cousin Charles when my father died. "Jules can always get a summer job here," he promised my mother. I could tell she thought not.

Cousin Charles handed out plastic bags of confetti to throw when the parade began and little American flags on wood sticks to wave. The mechanics grilled hot dogs and hamburgers for us and for their families. "Ben's going into the ROTC at the university this fall," Aunt Iris proudly told Aunt Joan, who didn't seem to hear, or care.

The parade, the marching bands with drums and trumpets that sounded first in your stomach and then in your ears, came grandly toward us down Main Street. "What do you want to be when you grow up, Jules?" asked Cousin Sarah, who, three years older than me, was my closest relation in age.

"I don't know," I answered.

"You have to know by the time you go to high school," she said. "You should be a scientist."

"I like drawing houses," I said as drums banged and marchers thundered past.

"That's called an architect," Cousin Sarah yelled above the sounds of the parade.

"Okay," I called back.

A band played "America the Beautiful." All of Goldenrod's fire engines, ancient and new, rolled by with their sirens blasting. Fantastic, floral floats were captained by the employees of some of the local shops. There was a theatrical salute to Yankee Doodle performed by the staff of the Harbor Shoe Store and a huge float of gold meant to be the Trojan Horse, courtesy of the Bonaventura Family Bakery. Pink-cheeked and sweaty, the Boy Scouts marched. Amid reveries red, white, and blue, smiling Girl Scouts strutted past. Sunlight glistened on the guns carried by veterans of all the wars who marched in the parade, including a very old man who saw action during the Civil War. We ate kosher hot dogs and hamburgers, brownies, and root beer.

I remembered my father died.

"Here she comes! Here she comes!" Mrs. Stanley exclaimed when she spotted Dana coming our way.

Dana Deamour, baton in hand, led the high school band down Main Street. She waved the baton back and forth; she wore a white, short majorette costume with opulent gold epaulets and bright, white boots with gold tassels. Her legs were, otherwise, bare and tanned from the long summer. Her blond hair was piled inside a gold and white hat with a brim and towering crown.

She was right in front of us now, her arm swinging high. She tossed the baton into the sky; we watched. It went so high my father could have caught it in heaven.

It fell; it hit the ground.

The crowd gasped. The baton rolled several feet away from Dana; her eyes caught mine. You heard the communal sigh; Dana's mother, Esther, went red with embarrassment. The high school band marched on. Dana froze. When the band had passed and Main Street was momentarily clear, Dana was gone.

My mother was asleep in her folding chair, a small American flag in her lap.

"There are lots of things you can be when you grow up, Jules," Cousin Sarah said, throwing confetti in the air.

TWENTY-THREE

. . .

I was ready to run.
Locked somewhere on a street in the borough of Queens with a
dead woman on the hood of the driving school Dodge, I was
ready for my great escape.

But no sooner had I unlocked the door and opened it just a
fraction than I felt something icy on the side of my neck. "Where
do you think you're going, faggot?" Hector asked.

He pressed the dolphin-silver revolver against me; I closed
the door.

"Good boy. Now get her off the fucking car!" Hector yelled.

"Please, Hector, no more," I pleaded.

" 'Please, Hector, no more,' " he imitated me. "I'll give you
more; just get her off the fucking car."

"Please, no!" I cried.

Hector cocked his gun; I believe that is the correct term. I
was officially out of my league now; what transpired next was
something from a movie. People who have been raped or as-
saulted always say that, if they live to tell the tale, but that is what
it is like. You are split out of yourself; you watch as if suspended in
front of a screen.

Hector's daughter covered her face with her hands; she didn't seem to have been hurt in the collision.

"Go on, pretty boy, get our girl off the fucking car," Hector insisted, the revolver now between my eyebrows.

My eyes watered; my contact lenses—a new pair put on just for the special occasion of my road test—blurred. "And what do I do with the body?" I whimpered.

"Leave it on the ground. Hurry up!"

"We can't leave it on the ground! We should call the police. Someone will have seen us. Someone probably has already called the police. They'll find us. You're the driving instructor—do I have to tell you it is a worse crime to hit and run than to hit and stay?"

Silence. Hector tickled the revolver from my forehead over my nose, along my shirt, and rubbed it in the crotch of my Armani trousers. "*Hello,*" he said. "Now, what words of my instructions did you not understand? Hurry up, faggot."

Should I have let him kill me? In a matter of minutes I would miss my column deadline, anyway; I would be as good as dead in the opinion of my editors. I got out of the car, looked for witnesses, saw none, and tried to pull the dead lady off the hood of the driving school car.

She wouldn't budge; I pulled again.

"Hurry up, faggot; get her off the goddamn hood and let's go!"

A high noon sun glistened on Hector's revolver. "Do I have to do everything myself? Can't you do a man's job?" he yelled, blood dripping from his lip.

I pulled and pulled; she didn't move.

"I'll count to ten," Hector said.

Eventually, I realized the woman was affixed to the windshield wipers. I put my hands under her chin, lifted her head, and was flooded in blood.

I removed her cushion of groceries. The last step was to unhitch the Wonder Bread from the windshield.

I pulled; she fell with a thud.

"Hurry up, get her out of the way!" Hector yelled.

I pulled her to the gutter and rested her head on some wet baseball cards and Chinese restaurant menus congealed over a sewer grate. I fixed her paisley dress so her knees were covered. I placed the jaunty hat over her face. Now I could run . . .

"Enough prissy-shit, man; get in the goddamn car," Hector said, the revolver aimed at me.

I got back in the car; I tried to wipe some of the blood off me.

"You drive," Hector said.

"What do you mean?"

"What do you mean what do I mean? I want you to drive. You wanted to learn to drive, so drive," he said. Hector, his revolver aimed at my head, got into the back seat of the car. "Sit in front," he commanded his daughter. She did as she was told. I took my place behind the wheel of the Dodge.

Hector rubbed his eyes. "Get going," he told me.

"Get going where?"

"Just drive."

"Please fasten your seatbelt?" I asked his daughter.

"Mind your own fucking business, faggot," Hector yelled and shoved the revolver into the nape of my neck.

I couldn't really see; the windshield was a spiderweb of shattered, bloodied glass.

"Turn the radio up," Hector said. "I like this song."

"I can't see – how can I drive? I can't see out the window."

"Turn the radio up, man, and just drive," he insisted.

I turned the radio up; the music was Ravel's *Bolero*.

"*Bolero?!* Deliver me," I said into the rearview mirror.

Hector tilted his revolver; I drove.

Hands fixed at ten-to-two on the steering wheel, always ten-to-two, I drove.

TWENTY-FOUR

...

For a while after my father died, especially during the months when she was decorating her new house, my mother was happy, I think, happy at least some of the time.

She certainly liked to laugh. For grown-ups, especially my older cousins, she reserved a salty sense of humor; this made them want to confide in her. They sought her counsel, and she obliged them willingly and generously, before she was slowed by the beginnings, and ends, of her illness.

Soon after we moved to the new house, a steady stream of visitors began calling. I remember one weekend afternoon coming in from wandering outdoors to find my mother in her kitchen intending to make a chicken for Cousin Gabby, who was expected to arrive by taxi soon from the train station in New London. Cousin Gabby, a fashion illustrator at *Harper's Bazaar* in New York, was the daughter of the eldest of my mother's four brothers, all of whom lived places other than Goldenrod.

"*Gotta* dance," my mother sang as I came through the door.

"Mommy?"

Before any paprika fell on the bird, my mother held it under its fleshy wings and danced around the kitchen. "The best dance partners, Jules, are the ones who don't talk," she laughed. My mother danced the chicken over the kitchen counter; she led it through a jig like a Highland fling.

"Let's name him before we cook him, shall we? What should we call him, Jules?"

I thought. "How about Mr. Shugrue?" I suggested, referring to my mother's omnipresent decorator.

"Oh, Mr. Shugrue, you say? Isn't that interesting, Jules. I thought you liked Mr. Shugrue." She sat the chicken on the counter's edge.

"He's okay," I said.

"But you wouldn't mind eating him for dinner. I understand," she smiled. "Okay, Mr. Shugrue, a very swell adieu to you," she said and rested the chicken on the spit of her new electric aluminum rotisserie.

We heard the taxi in the driveway. I ran to a front kitchen window and watched as my mother went to the door. Cousin Gabby and my mother were best acquainted by letters and occasional phone calls. Gabby was raised in Sarasota, Florida, where her father, my uncle Max, was a business manager for the Ringling Brothers Circus. (Years later, at his funeral, all the clowns came in full dress.)

"Let me just stand here, dear Auntie," I heard Cousin Gabby say. "The air! The air! It smells rich, Auntie, it smells rich!" she exclaimed in that way a certain generation of editors on fashion magazines have of saying everything, and nothing, in a few owl-like hoots and sweeping gestures.

"Sorry the place is still a mess; we've only just moved in. This is Jules, and that is Mr. Shugrue on the spit," my mother said when I met my cousin in the kitchen.

"Enchanted," Cousin Gabby sighed, giving me her hand to hold. "Oh, Auntie, oh, Auntie, you save my life with your delicious Goldenrod. The apple trees, the roses, the fertile country life, the honey in the air!"

"I'm afraid that is only paprika, darling. You do need a spell in the country, don't you?"

Something barked. From the top of an expensive satchel, Louis Vuitton, I later recognized, came the head of a small dog with a blue satin bow at its neck. "Meet Brutus, my darling little family," Cousin Gabby said.

My mother patted the Yorkshire terrier on its head; he growled. "*He* smells rich," my mother said. The women laughed.

I, of course, was intrigued by this visitor from New York. I remembered when my father took me to the train station in New London; New York City was where the trains went. My mother and I had already begun our early evening custom of reading the New York newspapers; she didn't like to cook, so we ate at Friendly's, the local outpost of a New England sandwich and ice cream chain. Adjoining our Friendly's was a drugstore that sold the out-of-town papers. We ate tuna melts and read all about life elsewhere. The around-the-town columns of Manhattan were especially satisfying, with their tales about people with names like D.D., Gloria, Babe, Slim, and Maggie; the giddy daily account-ings of their comings and goings were our soap operas. What a disappointment when we ate at home and missed that day's chronicle of our constant characters!

As Mr. Shugrue turned, so to speak, Cousin Gabby and my mother sat at the kitchen table; Cousin Gabby, who wore a black turtleneck sweater and trousers—the first time I'd ever seen a woman wear pants—showed us the latest issue of *Harper's Bazaar,* with her pencil ladies in French clothes. She said she went out every night and, on weekends and holidays, flew in planes with men. "I date actors," she said and sighed. "Don't tell Daddy!"

My mother and Cousin Gabby drank sherry in small crystal glasses. They smoked cigarettes; Cousin Gabby took her filterless Kools in a gold-and-tortoiseshell holder. Then, suddenly, and to my complete amazement, she systematically removed two tiny glass blue-tinted spheres from her eyes and placed them on the tip of her tongue.

"Contact lenses," she said, as if I knew.

I was still getting used to my first pair of eyeglasses. They were the first measurable change in myself after my father died; no tears, just eyeglasses. But what about those contact lenses? Weren't they the key to the something-for-everyone city, a brightly lighted future for all to see?

That night, I packed a brown bag with clean underwear and couldn't wait for the day I moved to the city where the trains went.

TWENTY-FIVE

...

Within, I suppose, about thirty minutes, thirty minutes of me driving into the more polite neighborhoods of Queens, despite the blood and the shattered glass that forbade any clear views, no less than seven police cars attended us in heated pursuit.

Sirens blared.

We would die now, for certain, I figured.

"Keep driving, faggot," Hector insisted, his revolver sentenced at the back of my head.

"Why don't you drive, Hector? Why don't you? I'm the guy without the driver's license; I can't see out the window. I don't know what I'm doing. I can't take this, I can't take this anymore. You drive!" I cried.

"I can't drive!" he yelled.

"What do you mean you can't drive?"

"I can't drive, faggot, I can't drive."

"Suddenly you can't drive? You got us into this mess driving, but now, suddenly, you can't drive?"

Hector's daughter squirmed next to me in the passenger's seat.

"Just drive, asshole, just drive!" Hector screamed. "If you don't, I'll kill you—I'll kill all of us!"

The police cars were getting closer. The sirens were deafening. "You drive, Hector," I said, "it's your last chance!"

"But I can't see!"

"What do you mean you can't see?"

"I said I can't see."

"What are you talking about?" I persisted.

"I said drive."

"I can't see, either; the windshield is a mess!" I yelled back.

"I need eyeglasses, asshole; they got broke last night," Hector muttered.

"What?"

"They got broke!"

"This is about eyeglasses?"

"Okay, okay, so I stepped on them myself last night. I walked into the kitchen wall when I woke up this morning and got this bloody nose. Okay, asshole? But that's why I couldn't work today; I can't see. I needed to get new glasses and I wanted my little girl with me. Don't you see, faggot! I've been driving us blind. Asshole! You fucking people, you goddamn suit-wearing New York motherfucking-faggot-assholes just don't get it. You think people like me are here just to get in your fucking way! To make you late! And you're ready to kill us for it, but not like we kill. We kill like men; you assholes want to play fucking faggot God! You threaten us with all your money and connections with all the assholes you know. Pussy boy doesn't get his license, he tells my asswipe boss he's going to write a mean article in some fucking two-bit fish-wrap newspaper. Fuck you! What the fuck's wrong with you, anyway? You want a license so fucking bad? Why didn't you do what every Pakistani dervish taxi driver and teenage motherfuck in this goddamn rathole town does? You get a fake license. You fucking idiot."

The police cars closed in. "I don't know," I said.

"You don't know?! Fuck you! You don't know. You're a real dumb fuck. That's the problem with you people; you don't know that you don't know. Get it: you threatened me; you threatened my daughter by thinking you could get me fired. Nobody does that, asshole, nobody!"

A police car pulled in front of us. I braked.

"Hector, I'm sorry."

"Yeah, me too."

"You got a driver's license?" an officer said, standing at my window, his hand squeezed on a pistol.

I didn't know whether I would laugh or cry.

The cacophony of police radio voices drowned out the radio; finally I could turn it off.

"Suspects are apprehended . . . deputy has accomplished traffic stop . . . suspect, Caucasian male, appears not to be armed . . . Hispanic male and female minor appear to be hostages . . . potential bias crime . . . deputy has approached vehicle," boomed a policeman's voice through a car radio.

Police surrounded the McCaulay's Driving School Dodge.

"Your driver's license," the officer at my window repeated.

"Officer, I can explain," I began. "You see, I don't have a driver's license."

I heard Hector, unseen by the policeman, cock his revolver.

"You're under arrest. New York State requires all operators of motor vehicles be licensed to drive. Get out of the car with your hands up," the officer demanded.

I wondered if it would help if I told him about my learner's permit, the one, I might add, that would expire within the week.

I said nothing; I didn't move.

I cringed when a policewoman opened the passenger's door to remove Hector's daughter from the car.

"Don't touch her!" Hector yelled. "Get your hands off."

The rest happened quickly, like in a movie.

A shot through the windshield; Hector had fired his revolver.

Spinning glass.

The police dived for cover.

I pushed Hector's daughter and myself out the door on her side of the car; we ran.

Two more shots.

Something tore through the trousers of my aforementioned Armani suit; I felt the blood burn on my leg. Hector's daughter and I ducked behind a gleaming Range Rover parked in the driveway of the nearest house.

Another shot; then silence.

"Surrender your weapon. Drop your weapon through the car window. Surrender your weapon and come out with your hands up," a policeman called through a bullhorn.

Hector's daughter covered her eyes.

Silence. No one moved.

I held Hector's daughter; I wanted to protect her. I wished I spoke Spanish; certainly, there were some pretty lies I could tell her to make her feel better.

Police helicopters and television news helicopters buzzed above us. Paramedics pulled up behind the police cars.

"Surrender your weapon," the policeman repeated.

With Hector's daughter secured in the cold-comfort embrace of my suit jacket, I peered from behind the Range Rover and could see her father. Hector sat upright, almost frozen, in the back of the McCaulay's Dodge; his revolver pointed at the ceiling.

How could I not have understood?

TWENTY-SIX

· · ·

President Kennedy was assassinated that November; I was nine years old. I watched the funeral, in black and white, on our color TV. Newscasters said the country was in shock; I wasn't. Fathers were dying that year; Mrs. Kennedy became the bellwether of our daily grief.

Almost daily new furnishings filled our new house. We were a family of things. As promised, my mother planned an extended trip to Miami Beach that winter. When I came home from school the afternoon before our intended departure, I heard voices from my mother's lavender bedroom; I recognized the sounds of my mother and a man. Her door was closed. "How could we? How could we ever have thought?" I heard my mother say.

The door opened.

I watched from the hall.

Mr. Shugrue walked past me; he stopped. "Take care of your mother," he said and left the house.

My mother stared at me; she buttoned her white blouse. "How long have you been standing there, dear?" she asked.

"Not long," I answered.

"How long?"

"Not long."

"I see," she said and lighted a cigarette.

I sat on her bed; she smoked. She brushed her auburn hair and regarded me from her mirror. "The decoration of houses is a complicated thing," she said and sighed.

"Blow smoke rings," I suggested.

"Smoke rings, indeed," she laughed and did her best, making concentric ripples of gray in the lavender room.

We ate at Friendly's, were entertained by reading the New York dailies, and came home to pack for the trip to Miami. I finished first, a suitcase filled with underwear my mother would repack in the morning. I looked in on my mother, and she had fallen asleep, still dressed, on her lavender bed.

Her sleeping scared me. It made me sad. We had a honeymoon, I think, after my father died; my mother buoyed by the reveries of our new house until, slowly, surely. . . . After all, my mother had been ill before my father; she took longer to die, that's all. I should have known; I should have understood. This wasn't a mystery; it was simply a function of time.

Uncle Israel, my father's most jovial brother, and his new, third wife, Gladys, came with us to Miami that winter. A car, with a driver, was hired to take us to the newly christened Kennedy Airport, formerly Idlewild, outside of New York City, about three hours from Goldenrod. One dressed for travel in those days. Uncle Israel, a tall man with a bald head and ghostly blue eyes, and I wore suits and ties; my mother and Aunt Gladys, in my mind a Yiddish version of a razzmatazz Gabor sister, all blond and bosomy, wore black suits, pearl earrings, and mink coats. Aunt Gladys, distrusting air travel and airline food, all quite new to us back then, had packed us a lunch in a wicker basket: bagels, lox, fresh fruit, and chicken sandwiches, each item elaborately wrapped in cellophane.

"There are germs in air-o-planes," she explained, as the hired car looped its way along the Connecticut Turnpike to Idlewild.

At the airport, porters took our suitcases, and we were led to the first-class lounge. My mother and I headed for a stack of New York dailies; Uncle Israel ordered a highball, although it was not yet noon.

"The mother's milk of the aged," he said and winked at me.

"Leah, look. Look!" Aunt Gladys said, excited. She pointed to a woman who had just arrived in the lounge followed by a trio of officious-looking men. The woman had enlarged, red hair; she wore a pink and blue tweed suit and an orange fox fur coat.

"Ethel Merman," Aunt Gladys purred.

"Is it?" my mother wondered.

"If that isn't Ethel Merman then my name isn't Gladys Moshen, er, Gladys Orr," my aunt said, forgetting her newest married name.

Uncle Israel raised his highball glass and laughed.

It was determined that it was Ethel Merman; we'd seen her on the *Ed Sullivan Show*. We boarded the plane in silence, all except Uncle Israel, who, feeling the effects of his highball, flirted with the stewardesses. Ethel Merman occupied the first two seats on the left side of the first-class cabin: one for herself, the other for her coat. My mother and I sat across the aisle; Uncle Israel and Aunt Gladys were in the row behind us.

The plane tumbled down the runway; we were airbound. There was the noise, the roar of the engines, the lift-off and wonder at the clouds penetrated by the plane. I remembered my father had died; where was he while we spoondrifted in the sky?

"Eat an apple, Jules? A nice chicken sandwich?" offered Aunt Gladys.

I declined; my mother was asleep.

Ethel Merman watched us; she patted the seat next to her, covered by her fur coat, and gestured for me to come sit. I did.

"Going to Miami?" she asked, folding the coat under her seat.

"Yes."

"Your mother?"

"My mother, yes," I answered.

"Pretty."

I studied my mother; she was still pretty.

"Wouldn't you like something?" Ethel Merman asked. "Some hot chocolate? Children like hot chocolate, don't they?"

"Okay."

A stewardess brought hot chocolate.

"My father died," I said.

Ethel Merman looked surprised. Her eyebrows, drawn in cocoa-brown pencil, went up. We tumbled through the clouds. Ethel Merman considered my mother's sleep. I drank the chocolate; I didn't know what else to say. "Your mother needs you," Ethel Merman boomed.

Did she?

"You mean right now?" I asked.

"No, doll, I mean she needs you all the time, center stage, curtain up!" Ethel Merman smiled.

Miami Beach has always been New York's East Village on water; now it is tattoos, models, black leather anything, big

pectorals and biceps, S & M lite, and tarty hotels. Then, it was all
water bagel-white buildings with citrus stripes, grandparents in
every shadow, the Yiddish theater. We encamped in a kosher
hotel; I was enrolled in a private day school in a coral mansion
that had once, I was told, belonged to the first Douglas Fairbanks.
You had to say "yes, ma'am," or "no, ma'am," to every question the
teachers asked; the students were dolphin mad, and a favorite
school outing was a trip to the Miami Seaquarium.

Aunt Gladys and my mother shopped for tropical-weight
shifts and beaded cashmere sweaters; Uncle Israel took me for
walks on Washington Avenue, a Borscht Belt bazaar of kosher
butchers and shops that sold carved coconut heads. We had our
pictures taken on Collins Avenue in front of painted screens of
pink flamingos and palm trees.

The Beatles came to Miami; my mother bought me a Beatles
wig made of black, absorbent cotton at the Woolworth's on
Lincoln Road, a shopper's strip where cars were not allowed.
I found a quarter left by prior guests in a vase in our hotel
room; in place of President Washington's head and the American
eagle were a showgirl's breasts and buttocks. Aunt Gladys took
me to see the film *Cleopatra;* "Look at those milk stations,"
Aunt Gladys said in the scene where Elizabeth Taylor bathes in a
warm pool.

The South Miami Beach sky was always bottle blue with
angel clouds; there were lizards and coral jewelry lost in the sands
and gardens. We went to wrestling matches at the Miami Convention Center; I got an autograph from a wrestler named Hay-
stack Calhoun.

"Julian! Julian!" I heard my mother scream on one of our last
nights in Miami Beach that winter.

We were in our hotel suite dressing for another kosher dinner. I ran from my room; I saw my mother crying. "What, Mommy, what is it?"

"It's lost, it's lost," she sobbed.

"What?"

"I can't find it, I can't find it."

"Can't find what?" I was panicked.

She stood in front of the dressing mirror; her hand stroked her throat. "My diamond heart is gone," my mother cried. "It's gone," she cried.

She had lost the diamond necklace my father gave to her; she sat on the edge of her bed and cried.

I tore the room apart looking for the diamond heart. I never found it. Uncle Israel and Aunt Gladys were called to help; so, too, were the hotel manager and staff. We never recovered the heart.

We returned to Goldenrod; my father had died. The reality of his death became the cleft in a world around which we skated, but it was never discussed.

Long silences. I made my own dinner or, in warm weather, rode my bicycle to Friendly's alone. I watched the new color television; I stopped drawing plans for new houses. My society, beyond fourth-grade grammar school, was Tuesday and Thursday afternoons at Hebrew school, where I hardly excelled. With so much unspoken at home, in English, Hebrew was just hieroglyphics and others' nuclear family trips to Israel.

My mother slept; sometimes she rallied and shopped. On occasion, if it was a Saturday, I might go along. That spring, because Cousin Kate had gotten a summer job after college at a Madison Avenue advertising company in New York, we drove, *en famille,* to New Haven, almost Manhattan, to shop for clothes for her to wear in the city.

My mother didn't care to drive; Aunt Joan, Kate's mother, enjoyed it. We left Goldenrod early that Saturday morning with Aunt Joan at the wheel. We drove past rural farms, toward the highway, to shop. Kate, all blue eyes and enthusiasm, and I sat in the back seat, behind our mothers. Kate had copies of the fashion magazines; they were our guidebooks: *Vogue, Bazaar, Mademoiselle, Seventeen.* "White boots, Courreges, Pierre Cardin, Norell, jumpsuits, oh, I want the new Revlon powdered blush-on," Kate said as she read.

"How's Phillip?" my mother asked.

"Dreamy," Kate answered, lost in *Vogue.* "Hmm, the pill . . ."

"Does he mind you working in New York this summer?" my mother wondered.

"I don't know. Maybe I don't really love Phillip, you know?"

"He's a good man, Kate; stick with the familiar," Aunt Joan said. "Why must you always reach for the moon?"

"Because the moon is reaching for me, Ma," Kate answered. "That's a line right out of the movie *Sabrina,*" she whispered to me.

The car was parked in a multilevel garage; we took an elevator to New Haven's outpost of Macy's. We gravitated, en group, to the cosmetics counter, where the women bought bottles of a bath oil called Youth-Dew, a new fragrance made by a lady named Estée Lauder.

"Jewish?" Aunt Joan asked my mother.

"I think so," she answered.

We'd read about Estée Lauder in the New York newspaper columns. This Estée Lauder was not only a friend of the D.D.'s and the Maggies, she entertained the Duchess of Windsor at her home in Palm Beach. "Look, we can get Estée Lauder makeovers and a free cosmetic bag," Aunt Joan said.

"Where are the A-line shifts?" Kate wondered.

A clerk even offered me a whiff of the Youth-Dew. I was intoxicated by the sweet-smelling potion. I wandered farther down the cosmetics counters; I looked up and my family was nowhere in sight. I remembered some talk about silk scarves and alligator handbags; I did not find the women at the counters where these things were sold. I looked and looked; I couldn't find them. Outside, it was raining. At the front door to the store shoppers rushed inside with their wet umbrellas pointed down like shotguns dripping after a jolly hunt. I figured if I stood outside, in front of the store door, my relations would find me; at some point they would look for me there.

Time passed. I leaned against the store window; there was a display of pink ladies' suits and flowered hats for spring and summer.

"I reckon you're lost," a store guard said.

I looked up into the gray eyes of the tall man in uniform; I nodded my head.

"Come on," he said and led me inside to a back elevator. Shoppers watched; they stopped and pointed. I was embarrassed. We took an elevator to a top floor and entered a room called Security; the guard poured ginger ale into a Styrofoam cup and gave it to me.

"Don't worry; don't cry, son," he said. "They'll come for you soon enough. They almost always do."

I waited; a radio played Broadway tunes. I drank the soda.

"You've got to try and always stick with your folks, son," the guard explained. "A department store like this is big, it's a version of the world, and you have to know where everything is, and where everything will be if there is a sale, before you can go off on your own. Stick with your own, unless you want to get lost."

The door to the Security room opened; Kate, my mother, and Aunt Joan were there. "Jesus, Jules, there you are," Kate said and took me by the hand.

"We're going home," Aunt Joan reprimanded. "Don't you ever do that again."

"Mother," Kate warned, trying to protect me from Aunt Joan's wrath.

My mother walked ahead to the elevator, which delivered us to the garage.

"I don't know, Aunt Leah, do you really think I'll wear white shoes in the city, even in summer?" Kate asked, talking nonstop about the clothing for sale in the store.

In the garage, my mother mistook a step; she started to fall. I don't know why, but she didn't raise her hands to block her descent; she fell in slow motion. Forever. When she hit the gray cement garage floor, she wept. A bottle of Youth-Dew tumbled from her shopping bag. Blood ran from her forehead; Aunt Joan and Cousin Kate rushed to her.

I'd never seen my mother sob like that before; it made me cry.

"I'm all right," she struggled to say. "I'm all right."

But she wasn't all right; we were not all right. Garage attendants and other shoppers gathered around us; I kept crying. Besides the cut on her forehead, my mother had twisted her ankle; everyone said she would be all right.

"Shut up, Jules, you've upset your mother enough for one day," Aunt Joan hissed when I wouldn't stop crying. She took her right hand and swung it back and then hit me on the side of my head; my eyeglasses slammed against my nose. But I stopped crying.

"I just think belted dresses if they are cut too loose are dowdy on a girl my age," Cousin Kate said as we drove away from New Haven.

That night at home, while we watched the color TV and my mother rested her ankle on an ottoman, I noticed around her neck my father's diamond necklace. "You found your heart!" I exclaimed.

My mother touched the necklace and smiled. "No, dear; I bought a new one," she sighed and closed her eyes.

TWENTY-SEVEN

...

Police radios, bullhorns, helicopters competed for attention in our impromptu, urban war zone.

Hector still sat in the back seat of the McCaulay's Driving School Dodge with his revolver pointed toward the ceiling of the car.

"Surrender your weapon!" called the police.

His daughter wrapped herself in my suit jacket in order to avoid seeing what was inevitably coming next. The cellular phone in my pocket rang. I didn't know if it was safe to answer; the police might confuse it for a weapon and shoot us.

The phone stopped ringing.

"Surrender your weapon!" the police blew through the bullhorn. More helicopters filled the sky like soiled seagulls before a storm.

The cellular rang again. I answered.

"Well," the familiar English voice purred, "do you have your driver's license?" Ines Spring asked.

"Geez, Ines, I don't know where to begin."

"Oh, Julian, you didn't fail did you?"

I stammered.

"You remembered the business of having your hands at ten-to-two on the steering wheel, didn't you?"

"Well . . ."

The helicopters and other cellular communicants mixed our line. I noticed on the bumper of the Range Rover behind which Hector's daughter and I were taking refuge was a sticker; "I'd Rather Be Reading Jane Austen," it said.

"Julian, I can't hear you; what's all that noise? What's going on? Why aren't you back in the office yet; haven't you got your deadline in a few minutes? We have a features meeting this afternoon at four, don't forget, and tonight we have that awful perfume launch at the Statue of Liberty. Where are you?"

The connection faltered.

"Ines, can you hear me? I think I might not make it to the office today; I think I might be on the news tonight, you'd better watch."

More interference; more police cars and helicopters.

"Julian, I've got to go upstairs," she said, meaning she was called to the offices of H.M., the man who owned *View*, among a number of other publications.

"Just make certain they mention *View* if you're on the news," Ines said.

"I'm afraid they probably will!" I yelled into the phone.

"Every little mention helps," she said.

Every little mention?

"Byeeee darling; hurry in."

TWENTY-EIGHT

...

Twelve years old. Besides bar mitzvah lessons I learned to dance.

A lady named the Widow Block held dancing and etiquette classes on Tuesday evenings at her home in Goldenrod for the children of the local gentry. The Widow Block's Victorian house was filled with tables and doilies, heavy oil portraits and photographs in silver frames that chronicled her ballroom dancing experiences around the world. "She was once a great beauty, the Widow Block," my mother told me.

Boys wore blue blazers, gray trousers, white shirts, and striped ties. Girls wore flouncy party dresses, patent leather Mary Janes, and white gloves. We sat on gilded chairs on opposite sides of the Widow Block's parlor.

"Children, children, children," the Widow Block exclaimed, her right hand pointed toward a chandelier, a busy charm bracelet drooled over her long, white kid glove. "You are about to embark on life's most daring, darlings, dare I say, adventure; to know how to dance is the key to everything: Civility! Society! Fraternity! Charm!"

Rusty foxtrot music played on an old Victrola.

"Charm, charm, charm . . . I cannot impress upon you too much the importance of charm in this world," she nearly sang.

There were lessons in waltzes, box stepping, foxtrotting, precociously energetic polkas, and the child-pleasing bunny hop. The Widow Block, her hair a teased beehive of silver and white, favored turquoise chiffon dresses with surfing necklines and blond boys for her dance partners. She would pull a boy off a gilded chair, hold him, and they would dance while the rest of us watched. Slipping momentarily into a reverie of charm and foxtrotting, she would recover in time to get the rest of us up and partnered on her parlor dance floor.

The good news was the punch; the girls poured for the boys.

The Widow Block insisted on clean shoes; we carried ours in plastic sacks to her house and changed footwear in the front hall. The goal for all those lessons was the spring cotillion at her house; she decorated with pastel streamers and white roses. There were two, instead of just the usual one, punchbowls of pink elixir and silver trays with butter cookies, raspberry drops, and cucumber sandwiches without crusts.

Parents were asked to wear dinner jackets and long dresses; the Widow Block wore a turquoise chiffon gown with a sheer pink train. My mother wore a long, navy blue dress with a firm white collar and cuffs and small rhinestone buttons.

"Boys, please ask your mothers to dance," the Widow Block announced midway into the cotillion.

I froze.

Slowly, I crossed the room and stood in front of my mother. She smiled. "Hello, Fred Astaire."

"Stop it," I said.

"Oh, darling," she said and opened her arms. "Let's face the music and dance."

I was only as tall as her bosom; I tried not to get lost there. My mother took my left hand; my right hand rested on her waist. We danced to the center of the room, which was, luckily, crowded so we did not have to box step much.

"Charm, charm, charm," I overheard the Widow Block say as she surveyed her room filled with mothers and sons dancing.

If I tried to look my mother in her eyes, as we had been taught, I stepped on her toes.

"It's all right, dear," she said.

"Talk about anything but the weather; talk about banking or romance," the Widow Block had taught us.

"Did my father dance?" I asked my mother.

"What did you say, Jules?"

"Did Daddy dance?"

"Oh, yes, it's good you learned how to dance, darling. Dancing is one of those quaint things that, when you no longer can do it, you can always remember."

"Charm, charm, charm," the Widow Block smiled as she glided by in the arms of a blond Goldenrod boy.

TWENTY-NINE

...

The police, to provoke Hector past the present impasse, aimed their guns at the tires of the McCaulay's Driving School Dodge.

They shot at all four tires; the car cooled to the ground, a dirge lost in a cough.

Hector, alas, shot back; his bullets sprayed in every direction.

"Suspect is shooting. Suspect is shooting to kill," announced an officer through his car radio beamed back to base.

Bullets ripped the turf; it sounded a razzmatazz of armored bells. A rat's meow. Hector's daughter held me tight; I looked at my watch. It was 2 P.M., my deadline exactly.

Hector jumped out of the Dodge; he shot his revolver in any direction.

The police returned the favor.

Bullets pumped back ten thousand times, unless I exaggerate.

Hector, a slow dance of blood, ran toward us behind the Range Rover. He was buoyed by the field of bullets; he kept running, his hands waving.

THIRTY

...

We saw a man drown once, my mother and I.

I was thirteen years old; it was the beginning of the summer when I was bar mitzvahed. My uncle Daniel had asked us to lunch at his place on the sound in New London. My mother and I went for a short walk on the beach before the meal; that's when we saw the man drown.

We noticed, in the distance, a commotion. Far enough away for us to feel separated, close enough to be unable not to see. A man in the water, his arms waving, his muted screams, and then nothing. Sunbathers ran toward the shore; another man dived into the water and swam toward him. He reached the drowning man; he held him in his arms and struggled to swim back to the sand. He breathed in his mouth for what seemed an eternity, then whispered:

"He's dead."

Ambulance attendants rushed to the scene. They covered the drowned man with a starched white sheet.

My mother stared ahead; she held her breath. We did not speak.

We returned to my uncle's terrace. Lunch was served. "What the hell's going on?" Uncle Daniel asked as he pushed open the screen door. He left us on the terrace and ran toward the crowd gathered on the shore.

My mother and I did not speak; we stared at each other like two animals in the dark foredoomed by a sudden, bright light. My mother lighted a cigarette and exhaled.

"Eat, Jules; why don't you eat something?" She glanced toward the platters of summer food – tomatoes, corn, grilled chicken breasts – on the white-clothed table.

"Uncle Daniel will say you ate anyway," she tried to smile and looked away.

THIRTY-ONE

···

Is he?" Hector's daughter asked.

"You speak English?" I responded, surprised.

"Yes," she said. "Is he dead?"

I didn't answer.

Paramedics and the police surrounded Hector's body.

"Is he?" She still hadn't turned to look.

"I think so. I mean, yes, probably; I'm so sorry."

The helicopters swooped closer. Newspaper people and television crews came next. There was a bedlam of questions and answers and microphones; we hid behind the Range Rover for as long as we could.

Hector's daughter had long, brown hair and dark, sad eyes. I guessed she was about seven or eight years old. "What's your name?" I asked.

"Ana-Luisa."

"And my name is Julian, Julian Orr. Why did I think you didn't speak English?" I asked.

Ana-Luisa shrugged her shoulders.

The paramedics checked to see if Hector might still be alive. The police photographers argued with the news photographers about who could get closer to the body. The rookies of each profession slipped in blood.

Ana-Luisa came out from the folds of my jacket and watched; I tried to stop her. I remembered myself at her age; I wanted to protect her. She held her breath; tears filled her eyes. "Is your mother at home?" I asked.

She shook her head no.

"Is she at work?"

Ana-Luisa shook her head no again.

An instinct told me the little girl's mother was not out of town on holiday. "Is your mother not alive?"

Ana-Luisa nodded yes, her mother was not alive.

"Have you any brothers or sisters? Grandparents? Aunts and uncles?

She whispered, "No."

The paramedics prepared Hector for the body bag.

"Maybe I should get your stuffed animal from the car," I offered. "Wouldn't you like that?"

Ana-Luisa didn't respond. She held me and wouldn't let go. Soon the police, and the press, would be all over us. We would be separated, Ana-Luisa delivered into the care of strangers. Same for me too, I imagined. Must it be that way? It occurred to me that this little girl could live with me, if she really didn't have any family. Wasn't that the least I could do? Take care of her and protect her? Maybe I could even adopt her. Why shouldn't we make a home together? Underneath our differences, we were two children with familial losses. I thought how wonderful it would be to spare her all the things I ever felt but did not want.

"What happens when your parents die?" Ana-Luisa asked.

I was stunned by the question, from just a little girl.

I thought I should explain to her that she was too young for me to really say, but how much more would I have preferred an answer to the question when I was her age. It is not knowing that eats at your confidence and carves the cleft in the world into which all your faith falls.

"I was nine when my father died and seventeen when my mother died," I said, not knowing how I might continue.

What happens when your parents die and you are still a child? What has happened is they have fallen, but they have fallen up. Priests and rabbis will tell you your parents have gone to heaven. So you look for them in the sky, in the morning sun, in every thunderstorm. You miss them; you wish they were here.

Policemen walked toward us. Concerned that we might be armed, they told us to put our hands above our heads. "The little girl, too," one of the officers barked when Ana-Luisa would not let go of me.

"Suppose you lived with me now?" I whispered to Ana-Luisa. "We can find you a really cool school, and, on Saturdays, we can go shopping and to the movies?"

Ana-Luisa shrugged.

"Hands up, you two; move it," a policeman repeated.

THIRTY-TWO

. . .

Mom Drops Tot in Falls," read the headline in the *New York Post* that day.

"Teenager Attempts Suicide While Neighbors Cheer," said a smaller headline on the same front page.

The newspaper rested on a chair outside the rabbi's office at the synagogue in Goldenrod. It was a mid-June summer morning; school was out, but I was there to be tutored for my bar mitzvah at the end of the month. The lesson was over—the Hebrew portion of the Torah I was to read on the appointed Saturday morning had been spelled out for me phonetically in English—but it was too hot to wait for my mother outside.

"May I read your newspaper?" I asked Mrs. Breitbart, the rabbi's secretary.

"Ask your mother," Mrs. Breitbart grumbled.

"Ask my mother?"

"That story? It's not the sort of story for a pre–bar mitzvah boy, if you ask me, and you did. So ask your mother."

Mrs. Breitbart churned a cigarette between tar-stained, red-nailed fingers. Smoke bounded off her helmet of black hair with a flip. Her desk was right in the middle of a Star of David on the office linoleum floor; at least the room was air-conditioned. The cold air fluttered the pages of one of Mr. Pitt's calendars; practically everyone in Goldenrod had a calendar from Mr. Pitt, especially the Jewish families. Mr. Pitt was the town's leading insurer; he loved his Jewish customers. "The Jews worry so much," I once heard him explain to my mother when he called on some business.

The horn of my mother's new, blue, air-conditioned LeMans blew; I ran to the car. "Can we have lunch at Friendly's?" I asked.

"No, I want to go home. I'm tired, dear."

"I want to get a copy of the *New York Post;* there's a story on the front page, 'Mom Drops Tot in Falls,' which Mrs. Breitbart said I shouldn't read."

"She said that?"

"She did."

"Thank you, Mrs. Breitbart," my mother sighed as she drove through Goldenrod toward home.

"What is the story about?"

"Does it look like it might rain, Jules?"

"Mom!?"

My mother drove. She took the route that led past my father's old Pontiac garage—Cousin Charles had located elsewhere with triple the space—and past our old house and neighborhood. This produced a moment, if not a chasm, of silence. "Jules, do you know the facts of life yet?"

"The facts of life?"

"About the birds and the bees?"

"Sure," I answered and lied.

"Good."

"Why?"

"Well, Jules, 'Mom Drops Tot in Falls,' it's a painful case — which also, so you know, is the name of an excellent short story you might want to read. I told you Dana Deamour would come to no good someday, didn't I?" my mother asked.

I assumed she was changing the subject again, but she wasn't. "Mom Drops Tot in Falls" was the story of Dana Deamour, whom I had seen perhaps but twice, and not in at least three years, since my father died. I knew that Dana had moved to New York City and had married; her husband, an artist, left her soon after her baby was born last year.

"I might as well tell you about it," my mother said. "It's the talk of the town. I stopped at Mrs. Stanley's on my way to get you this morning; she told me the story and she had copies of the New York papers."

Dana Deamour was left by her husband — "if they ever were really married at all," my mother commented — in a nondescript tenement building on Manhattan's Lower East Side. There were cats' cries, wives' cries, city cries, and Dana's baby's cries. Added to that were the cries of a seventeen-year-old boy, a vagrant, who lived illegally in a room down the hall from Dana Deamour's. Dana imagined he was an Italian prince, or an actor, someone between appointments, much like herself.

The baby cried all the time. Dana's solution was to take the baby for walks in the city, where the sounds of the town drowned out the child's crying. The baby was already seven months old and Dana had yet to name it; she hoped her husband might come back and then they would choose a name. Until then, Dana called her son her Maybe Baby.

"Mrs. Stanley and Esther had lost touch with Dana; she didn't have a phone, and they doubted their letters reached her," my mother explained. "Sometimes, on a Sunday from Grand Central Station, Dana would call home collect. She was always carrying on about this man and that man and a job she expected to get in Hollywood, the poor girl. Sometimes a woman isn't quite right after she has a baby, Jules, her mind goes rather queer."

The day before the accident, Dana awakened with a desperate need to stock her medicine cabinet with every imaginable lotion, bandage, and elixir—things she might never use but wanted for safekeeping nonetheless. She secured the Maybe Baby in this sort of knapsack, a contraption that suspends a child in a cotton cocoon over one's bosom, and walked to the nearest drugstore, stopping on her way to cash her last check from a job she had held as a switchboard operator at a midtown hotel.

"The drugstore, if you can imagine, was called Love's," my mother said. "This was written in the newspaper. Journalists, darling, call this a 'detail.' "

Dana Deamour bought bandages in all sizes, antiseptic cleaning agents for cuts and scrapes, an eye cup, eye wash, a burn ointment, calamine lotion to relieve minor itches and rashes. She bought petroleum jelly, antifungal powder, spray to stop athlete's foot, and a sunscreen for the baby's head. She bought a syrup of ipecac to induce vomiting. She bought potions to stop it. She bought surgical tweezers with a built-in magnifier to remove splinters. She bought sterile cotton balls, blunt-end scissors for cutting gauze, an elastic bandage for strains, aspirin, acetaminophen for people who cannot take aspirin, "just in case her teenage neighbor was one of those people," my mother said.

"Of course, Dana, being Dana, also bought herself a new lipstick called Hot Frost." My mother shook her head and headed the LeMans toward home.

When Dana returned to her building, the teenager was sitting on the stoop sweating out the hot summer's day. "It struck her all at once, when she laid eyes on the poor boy, that she knew what her life was all about. 'True love is my destiny,' she actually told the police who would later arrest her. Only Dana Deamour would say something like that," my mother continued.

"You want to come with me to Niagara Falls?" Dana asked her neighbor. "It's going to be cooler there."

"You going?"

"Go if you go."

"Haven't got the money."

"I got the money if you'll come," Dana offered.

They decided to leave that night; Dana rushed across the street to a pay phone and called the Port Authority for the bus schedule for departures to Niagara Falls. "I have some clothes you might like to try," she told the neighbor. "Upstairs, my husband's things."

The teenager shrugged; he followed Dana inside the molting tenement.

The pale blue suit and brown acetate shirt didn't fit; he wore them anyway. The neighbor held the Maybe Baby almost all the way to Niagara Falls, and the child never once cried. "Only more evidence, as far as Dana was concerned, that true love was her destiny," my mother said.

"Oh, Jules, I wish you were old enough to drive. It's much more fun to ride," my mother sighed, stopping for a red light near a dairy farm.

The only trouble with the neighbor holding the baby all the time was that his hands weren't free to hold Dana's. "She told that to a reporter, too," my mother said, continuing with the story. "She finally got around to asking the teenager his name. It was Gabriel Lennon; right there and then she named her Maybe Baby Gabriel after the boy."

They arrived at Niagara Falls shortly after sunrise. It was a glorious day; Dana took the baby from her neighbor and sent him off to buy them some refreshments. But the minute she held the baby, he began to cry. She tried to stop him; she tried to explain that this was the most important day in her life—in their lives—because today she and her true love would meet their destiny. "And they certainly did," my mother said.

My mother parked the LeMans in the driveway of our house; she dropped the car keys into her alligator bag and snapped its gold clasp closed. "As Dana was explaining all this to the baby, to make him stop crying, she found herself walking closer and closer to the falls themselves. She walked much too far out; the teenager saw her from a distance and ran to stop her. Dana was overcome with vertigo and the screams of the crying baby; the boy grabbed her by the back of her blouse, but it was too late. To block her ears against the sound of the baby's cries, Dana had opened her arms and, of course, the baby fell.

" 'Mom Drops Tot in Falls'; you saw the headline, Jules. 'The baby was pulled by angels into the violet sky,' Dana told a reporter. The poor dear, the poor child." My mother shook her head.

"What happened to the boy?" I asked.

"After being questioned by the police, he went back to New York and climbed to the roof of the tenement and almost jumped. The neighbors cheered him on, but the police in New York stopped him."

I followed my mother into our house. "And Dana?" I asked.

"She is under supervision in a mental hospital in upstate New York; it's doubtful she will ever live anywhere else for the rest of her life," my mother explained. "Mrs. Stanley would like it if she could at least be transferred to the state hospital here; you know the one, it's next to the cemetery where your father is buried. Can you get your own lunch, Julian? I want to read for a while."

My mother settled herself in her favorite chair in the family room; I made a sandwich and picked at the bread. I looked in on my mother; she had fallen asleep, her auburn hair fanned out against the back of the chintz-covered Queen Anne chair, the novel she was reading toppled on the floor.

"Don't lose my place," she said, waking up briefly when I closed the book and put it on a side table.

I knelt in front of my mother's chair and rested my head in her lap. She smoothed my hair with her hand. "What's the matter, Jules, are you ill?"

She closed her eyes to sleep again; I mouthed the words "I love you."

My mother slept.

It was early afternoon, and I went for a bike ride. Instead of my usual route, however, I rode toward the cemetery where my father was buried. I had been there only once since he died; I wanted to see his grave. We drove by it often enough—on shopping trips to the other side of town—and my cousin Sarah and I would raise our feet, something we were told one was meant to do when passing a graveyard.

I figured it would be a long bike ride—about an hour at least. I rode and rode, until I saw the state hospital at the crest of a hill, a series of redbrick buildings peering incongruously over the elm and maple trees that hid the Jewish cemetery. It was eerie, of course; the windows of the hospital were open because it was summer. You heard voices and cries through the bars at the windows. I leaned my bike against a tree; I found the best stone I could to put on my father's gravestone. It's a Jewish tradition; that way the dead know you have come calling. The gate to the cemetery was unlocked; when I was inside I couldn't remember which was my father's grave. There were Goldbergs, Goodmans, Cohens, Steinbergs, Steins, but I could not find the Orrs.

At the far side of the graveyard, near a stone wall, I noticed an amber tree.

I walked toward it almost as if I were in a dream. I imagined I heard my father's voice. "Dear son, dear son," it said.

I walked nearer to the amber tree; there were two men digging a grave. "It's him," I thought one said.

"Him?"

"His son," the first man repeated and pointed.

"Oh, his son? But for the grace of God go we," I think they sang.

"Do you know where my father is buried?" I called. "My father," I said, "Saul Orr."

The gravediggers raked; they didn't hear me. I turned and walked toward the amber tree. I could not find my father's grave. When I looked back toward the gravediggers, they were gone.

I never did find my father's grave that afternoon, although I walked row after row looking. It was getting late; I wanted to get home to my mother.

I found her still sleeping in her chair. My return awakened her; she opened her eyes and smiled.

"Hungry?" she asked.

I nodded my head yes.

"Friendly's?"

"Yes, please," I answered.

Despite both my and my mother's suspicion that I was not becoming an average statistical man, I was bar mitzvahed in a rose-and-lilac-filled temple that summer.

All the guests, all the relations, said they wished my father were there.

THIRTY-THREE

. . .

Okay, you two, hands up. Put your hands over your heads and spread your legs against the jeep. You have the right to remain silent . . ."

"Officer, there's been a terrible mistake; I should explain everything," I said, turning around.

He pulled his revolver from its holster; we did as we were told and splayed ourselves against the car.

"I'm not going to cry," Ana-Luisa mumbled.

"It's okay; maybe you should. I might," I whispered.

"Quiet, you two," the police officer said.

My cellular phone rang; several rings later it stopped. It rang again; it stopped. It rang again.

"Okay, answer your phone," the officer allowed.

"Hello, hello!" I could barely hear the person at the other end; the helicopters and sirens were that loud around us.

"Darling, are you all right?" It was Ines. "What is going on? H.M. told me you were already on the news. An accident? You took someone hostage? That's what they are saying."

"How is everything there?" I asked, uncertain if I should tell the story of the morning to Ines while the policeman listened.

"Oh, you know, Julian. We have Linda, Christy, and Naomi with Steven in Oyster Bay for a cover try and it looks like rain; business as usual. Now what is going on?"

"I am in a bit of a fix, I'm afraid; Ines, I need a good lawyer."

"What about your agent—isn't he a lawyer?"

I pictured my agent, Zab Hammer, to whom I was late with payments for the commission he took from my newspaper and magazine salaries, and couldn't imagine he was the man to call. "I'm late with my commission checks," I yelled into the phone. "I don't think Zab Hammer is the solution."

"I'll call Eddie Bankhead for you," Ines said. "What should he do?"

"I suspect I'll be taken into police custody; I can't say any more, if you know what I mean. Eddie should find out what precinct I'm taken to and meet me there. There's a little girl involved, too."

Eddie Bankhead was a good idea. He was the son of a Bronx policeman who rose up through the ranks, socially as well as professionally, when he became the inspiration for a novel by Tom Wolfe.

"Julian, what exactly happened? Did you get your license or not?" Ines asked.

"Not," I sighed.

"I'll call Eddie," Ines promised. "And Julian?"

"Yes."

"Play down your connection to *View,* will you? For H.M.'s sake; he hasn't been in a good mood lately."

"Yes, sure," I said.

We hung up. "How you doing?" I asked Ana-Luisa.

She didn't answer.

In the minutes that followed we were searched and questioned about the painful case; I kept saying I wouldn't answer until I consulted with my lawyer. "The same goes for the little girl," I said.

Hector was pulled into a body bag; Ana-Luisa closed her eyes.

Three officers hoisted him into an ambulance; it sped away. A blue police car pulled up; a lieutenant got out of the passenger's side, and I recognized him as he walked toward us. It took me a few minutes to realize how I knew him. Then it hit me: he was the lieutenant who, earlier that year, had created a local sensation by posing, out of uniform, of course, for *Playgirl*. I didn't think it was entirely appropriate, or useful, considering the circumstances, that an image of this fellow buck naked on the hood of an NYPD police car flooded my mind. "That's Not a Gun in His Pocket," squealed the *Playgirl* headline.

The lieutenant, three times my size in every direction, didn't seem happy to see us. "So what the fuck happened here?" he asked and ran a hand through his jet black hair.

"Lieutenant?"

"I said, what the fuck happened here? You obviously have been on some kind of joy ride this morning. And let's see: we have one woman dead, somebody's grandmother, I might add, and we have one man dead, somebody's father, I see."

"I can explain," I said nervously.

"Please do." The lieutenant leaned against the police car and rubbed his thighs. He crossed his arms over his chest and awaited my explanation.

"Well, sir, I've been learning to drive."

"What?"

I tried not to remember the *Playgirl* spread. I recalled that the lieutenant was amply uncircumcised; the magazine had made a big deal of that relative novelty.

Ana-Luisa squeezed my hand; she was trying not to cry.

"I've been learning to drive," I continued. "I was meant to have my road test today, but we never quite got to the Motor Vehicle Department in Sheepshead Bay. We got lost; the driving instructor, Hector, the man who is dead, well, we got into a little scrap, and then . . ."

Ana-Luisa began to sob. I held her hand as tight as I could without hurting her.

"All right, pal," the lieutenant said. "It's time we go for a ride."

Ana-Luisa and I were led into the lieutenant's car; there were reporters on the scene, yelling questions. The lieutenant wrapped his arm around Ana-Luisa and me and guided us into the back seat of his car; he smelled of Brut cologne and police station cigarettes. A policeman drove; a policewoman rode in the passenger's seat in front. Seven police cars followed us toward town; sirens blasted the entire way. Eventually, we left Queens, and the Manhattan skyline, drawn in near rain, loomed forward like a diehard cynic's Oz.

"Those bruises look pretty bad," the lieutenant said.

I'd forgotten them; luckily the bullet that tore my trousers apart had left as quickly as it had come. My leg burned, but I was not struck lame. I raised myself in the back seat of the police car to look at my face in the rearview mirror; I looked like a tomato kicked off a farmstand cart.

"Sit down," the policeman driving said.

"I'm not a pretty sight, am I?" I asked Ana-Luisa and squeezed her hand. "We forgot my friend's stuffed animal in the driving school Dodge," I said.

"It'll be among the evidence at the station," the policewoman in the front said.

"Lieutenant," I began, "perhaps I should introduce myself."

"Don't bother," he said. "I know who you are; my girlfriends read the *Tribune*. All them parties you go to, some fancy life. Who would have thought it?"

"Thought what?"

"Save it for the station."

"Listen, lieutenant. I think if you let me explain what happened today, you will see what we have here is a painful case, verily the stuff of New York, I'm afraid, and. . . ." He didn't seem the least bit interested.

I looked out the window; we were ushered through the toll booths at the Midtown Tunnel. "I'm worried about this little girl," I told the lieutenant.

"You should be. We're contacting her next of kin," he said.

"But I don't think she has any; she is an only child, there aren't any relations, she says. Isn't that right, Ana-Luisa?"

She shrugged.

"If there is no next of kin, then family court will place her in an appropriate foster home," the lieutenant said.

"I would like Ana-Luisa to stay with me."

"Not a chance," he said.

"Why not?"

"You can apply for the foster parents' program, but it is not as easy as you think. They aren't partial to, well, singles, if you know what I mean."

"You mean gay people?"

"You said it, not me."

I was angry. "Listen, lieutenant, how about cutting me some slack? This has been a really shitty day, so far. We've all got our problems; we've all been in some fairly sticky situations." I remembered that soon after his *Playgirl* spread came out, what really annoyed his superiors was when the lieutenant, flushed with the publicity, attended a gay organization's fundraiser; he wore only a Speedo swimsuit and his badge.

"You saw my *Playgirl* spread?"

"Why, yes, I did. I even saved it," I lied.

"Far out. Yeah, got me into some kind of hot water," he said as we drove west on Thirty-eighth Street. "I had to peel the lonesome off me, let alone every fruit fly from here to Hoboken."

The police officers in the front seat exchanged disapproving looks. Amid a field day of sirens we arrived at the precinct house on West Fifty-fourth Street. The lieutenant ushered Ana-Luisa and me from the police car; there must have been one hundred reporters and photographers waiting for us.

"Hey, Julian, what's a nice society writer like you doing in a mess like this?" one reporter yelled as we rushed inside the police station.

"Come on, Julian," a woman called, "meet the press; we're your makers."

"Whatsamattuh, Julian? Too good to talk? Saving your story for a *Tribune* exclusive: 'What We Wore on our Deathride through Queens'?" yelled another.

The reporters laughed; cameras flashed.

My mind, meanwhile, raced with my plan to keep Ana-Luisa with me. The more the obstacles presented themselves, the reasons the lieutenant had described that I could not keep her, the more determined I became. The events of the day had forged a lifelong bond between us; I did not want to let her go. To win, I would have to manage the following in swift order:

Call my editor at the *Tribune* and see if they still wanted me to file a column for tomorrow's paper; it was already after three o'clock, an hour past my deadline.

Try and make the features meeting at *View* at four.

Prepare a bed for Ana-Luisa; find a babysitter for tonight if I was still to go to the perfume launch as Ines expected.

Bury Hector.

Find a school for Ana-Luisa in the neighborhood; wasn't Brearley the best?

Get a driver's license.

Drive to my parents' graves.

Find out how much television Ana-Luisa could safely watch; what did she like to eat?

Learn to cook.

Buy Ana-Luisa new clothes.

Save money for her college education.

Ana-Luisa held my hand as we followed the lieutenant to his office. The precinct house seemed a question mark of confusion; there were clouds of cigarette smoke and empty coffee cups, phones ringing, radios.

"Sit here," the lieutenant said, indicating two metal chairs outside his office.

I looked for a sign of Eddie Bankhead. "Are you hungry?" I asked Ana-Luisa.

She shrugged neither yes nor no.

"You should eat," I said and asked the lieutenant if we might order lunch.

"You want too much," the lieutenant said.

"Lunch, lieutenant," I responded rather shrilly, "for a child. A simple child!"

"All right, all right. I'll send an officer over with a menu from the coffee shop. But I can't believe you're thinking about food when you're up for murder charges. Only a guilty man thinks of food at a time like this," he said and closed his office door.

Murder? Me?

I caught the eye of the lieutenant's assistant, a large white woman who wore jeans and a Madonna "Like a Virgin" concert-tour T-shirt. "Love your column," she said and sneezed.

"A cold?"

"Bad office air," she said and blew her nose.

Phones rang; officers rushed by.

"Everything will be all right," I promised Ana-Luisa, who sat silently next to me.

"Do you think I can use my cellular phone?" I asked the lieutenant's assistant.

"Unless someone stops you," she said.

I dialed Hap Shragis, my editor at the *Tribune*, and got his voice mail. I left a message for him to call me on my portable. A radio on the assistant's desk played the local news. The newscaster reported the latest health care debate in Washington; the hit-and-run killing by an errant driving school car of a grandmother in Queens—my name was mentioned; my stomach ached—and a story about the illegal immigration to the United States of Haitian boat people. "Parched," the radiocaster said, "they, the boat people, mistake the water for earth and they think of their mothers and think they can walk. They walk, but then they drown, on the sea, under the punishing sun. No one can walk on water . . ."

"What happens when your parents die?" Ana-Luisa asked.

"Ana-Luisa, darling," I said, "I know it's hard, but try to rest; everything will be okay. I promise."

She closed her eyes; I held her hands. What else happens when your parents die, I thought.

The world slices open.

You freeze in the sun.

The cellular phone rang; it was Hap Shragis.

"Hey, Scoop," he called into the phone.

"Scoop?"

"You're the top of the news, man, way to go. A banner headline on tomorrow's edition, Julian."

"Now, Hap, I called to apologize for missing my deadline; you know I'm pretty good, usually, may be late a few minutes once in a while. I'm really sorry about tomorrow's column."

"Relax, relax. You've got until nine tonight to file; we're giving you the front page, and we'll jump the copy to your page. No sweat."

"But Hap, I doubt I can write about what happened today; I'm a suspect in a murder. Isn't that a conflict of interest?"

"Stuff of tabloid dreams, Julian, stuff of tabloid dreams."

"Please, Hap, can't I have the day off?"

"Write the story big, Julian: big, big, big . . . let yourself roar."

"But, Hap, I can't; I don't want to."

"You've been covering too many perfume launches, Julian, you've lost sight of real news. This is your chance."

"My chance to what?"

"To show the new management here that you're not a wuss."

I was silent.

"You there, Julian?"

"I'm here."

"Let me level with you. You and me we're friends, but the new management? Well, they aren't what you'd call gay-friendly. I'm sorry, but they aren't. The powers that be down here aren't loving you. Face it, Julian, it's the big, bad world. This is just the scoop you need. Write your story. Show them."

"I quit."

"You can't; you're under contract until October."

I knew there wasn't any point in arguing anymore. "All right, Hap, you'll have my copy by nine."

"Good boy. What are you covering tonight, by the way? Do we need to send a photographer?"

"I'm covering a perfume launch," I said.

"Will there be any supermodels?"

"I suppose," I answered.

"Well, for your sake, and mine, catch 'em in a catfight!"

"But, Hap, these girls aren't like that. They're top-drawer professionals who just do their jobs."

"Ahhh, Julian, you're writing yourself out of the best job you're ever going to have."

He hung up.

"My brilliant career," I smiled at Ana-Luisa.

She gave me a curious look.

We waited. Finally, down the aisle between the police officers' desks came Eddie Bankhead, tan with gray-blond hair, shaking hands and saying his hellos; he seemed to know everyone. Despite his imposing swagger, and accent, which was all Bronx, his look was one hundred percent Savile Row: he wore a chalk-striped suit—rust-colored stripes on charcoal gray, to be precise—a vest, a gold watch on a chain, a straight-collar pale yellow shirt, a pink-and-blue club tie, and laced-up brown suede saddle shoes.

"Man, are you in a fucking mess," he said and plunked himself down on one of the metal chairs outside the lieutenant's office.

"Eddie," I said, "this is Ana-Luisa, the daughter of Hector, the man who was killed from the driving school today."

Eddie Bankhead spread his legs and crossed his arms over his chest. "How you doing, Ana-Luisa?"

She didn't answer.

"Can you get us out of here, Eddie?" I asked.

"Patience, Julian, patience." He shook his head. "Ana-Luisa, sweetheart, how old are you?"

"I will be eight next week."

Eddie shook his head. "Julian, have you seen the press outside?"

"Yes, on the way in."

"So what happened?" he asked.

I told him everything, the story of our day, beginning with Ines and I deciding we would learn to drive. I even told him why I bothered, so I could visit my parents' graves.

"Helluva story," he said. "The problem is, the police think you killed the grandmother. They think you were driving and you hit and ran."

"Was I driving?" I asked Ana-Luisa.

She shook her head no.

"Terrific," Eddie responded. "An alibi supported by a seven-year-old."

"Eight next week," I said.

Ana-Luisa slouched in her chair.

"Furthermore, Eddie, I want the family court to give me custody of Ana-Luisa. She doesn't have any family; I don't want her put in a foster home. I want to raise her."

"No living relatives?" Eddie asked Ana-Luisa.

"No," she whispered.

A newspaper photographer took our picture.

"Get him out of here!" Eddie yelled.

A police officer removed the photographer.

The lieutenant's office door swung open. "Fucking A! Somebody get this goddamn bird out of my office!" he yelled.

A sparrow had wedged itself inside two panes of window glass. Three officers came running; one got a broom and jabbed at the window.

"Eddie," the lieutenant said, shaking the lawyer's hand.

"Tommy, buddy, how you been?" Eddie Bankhead stood and wrapped his arms around the lieutenant.

"You his lawyer?"

"Lawyer to his boss. Just helping out, you know," Eddie explained. "Man, I haven't seen you in a coon's age, not since that story in *Playgirl*. Way to go, man."

"Still in some hot water over that here. But, hey, you saw it?"

"My girlfriend had it; made me not want to take my clothes off for three weeks, pal."

The lieutenant laughed. A good sign, I hoped.

The camaraderie ended; the lieutenant got down to business. "We're talking manslaughter, Eddie. Your boy here is going to be charged with manslaughter. 'Society twit,' no offense intended, 'plows down black grandma,' " he said, forecasting future newspaper reports. "Some headline for a city that only has one story: race."

The lieutenant walked back into his office to see how the police officers fared getting rid of the sparrow. "Come on, guys," he complained, "hurry up. Just shoot the goddamn bird!"

"Don't you dare," insisted his assistant.

"Tommy, Tommy, let me tell you a story," Eddie Bankhead called after the lieutenant. "Sit down." He gestured to an empty seat. "Tommy, it's a story about transportation and all its mysteries, which is at the heart, at the very quintessence, of what happened to my client today."

"Oh, yeah? How so?" wondered the lieutenant.

"Picture it: Indonesia, and the good, Islamic people of that country," Eddie Bankhead began. "Now, as you know, Tommy, it is the spiritual mission of these people to get themselves, at least once in their lives, to Mecca. It is their pilgrimage, Tommy, so they can circle the holy shroud at least once before they die. It is their reason to live.

"Now, Mecca, as you also know, is somewhere in the Middle East. Somewhere, don't ask me the fuck where, but it's somewhere over there in the Middle East. Wherever it is, it is fucking far away from Indonesia. But that doesn't stop these good people; for centuries they have traveled by foot, camel, caravan, sea, whatever it takes to get to the Holy Land. This requires faith, Tommy, faith, leaps of faith," Eddie continued.

He paced the antechamber, his arms raised and lowered for emphasis as he told this story. I could not imagine the point. Ana-Luisa was more interested in the police officers trying to unwedge the sparrow.

"Get a clear picture, a very clear picture, Tommy, of the struggle of these people to get to Mecca," Eddie said. "Rain, wind, sleet, and I don't what the hell else. Snow? Drowning sands? Torrential winds, loneliness. Imagine the faith this requires. The old-fashioned route to Mecca took years, Tommy, fucking years, but here comes the screw, the modern screw.

"Some smart-ass entrepreneurial type hears about these roving masses and decides to make a 747 Boeing available for them to charter. The jet will get them to Mecca in a matter of hours instead of years. Instead of saving all their money and packing their belongings in some hairshirt suitcase, they can give their money to their village leaders and fly to Mecca. Not that they have a clue what an airplane is, but they trust their leaders; they pay, they prepare, they sign a waiting list.

"Finally, their turn comes. They pack their belongings; the pilgrimage begins. They light candles; they pray all the way to the airport, not that they know what the fuck an airport is. It's all about faith, Tommy, you're empowered by your belief. And when you get to the airport and are directed toward this silver bird, well, you think that's Mecca. You sing hallelujah! You board the plane, climb the stairs with your lighted candles. You take your seat; you think you're in Mecca.

"You light more candles; some stewardess in a tarty little dress tries to blow them out. You relight the candles. Soon engines roar. The captain speaks. Is it Mohammed? It's bedlam: the stewardesses trying to blow out your candles, the captain's voice. The 747 roars down the runway and takes off; it's terror. This is Mecca? The passengers shit in their seats."

We heard glass shatter. "Okay, boss, sorry about that, but we had to break the window to let the bird out; he's gone," reported one of the policemen.

"Good," the lieutenant sighed.

Eddie Bankhead, not one to be upstaged, held forth. His eyes burned into the lieutenant's.

"What's your point, Eddie?"

"My point, Tommy, is this: Man plans, and God—or Mohammed or whomever you pray to—laughs," exhaled Eddie Bankhead. "My client here was simply trying to learn to drive. He wanted a license so he could drive home. He is innocent of every crime you have imagined of him, every crime, except the crime, which it isn't, Tommy, of wanting to go home again."

"Let's you and me have a private chat, Eddie," the lieutenant said and got up and walked into his office.

The door closed.

Ana-Luisa and I waited.

About thirty minutes later the door opened. Eddie Bankhead, standing on the threshold, looked pleased.

"I got you off," he said. "No charges will be filed."

"That's it?" I asked.

"I promised the lieutenant you'd mention him from time to time in your column. Here's a list of names of his girlfriends you should send subscriptions to of *View*. Let's go; you should see a doctor about that face. You look bad," Eddie said.

"What about Ana-Luisa?"

"If you really want to keep her, you'll have to convince the family court. An officer will be here soon; you can wait if you like. It's not going to be easy," Eddie said.

"I want to keep her," I said and took Ana-Luisa's hand.

"Suit yourself. I'll send my bill to you at the office." Eddie swaggered down the aisle of the police station and met the press outside.

175

Soon a heavyset woman with a swamp of red hair approached. "Hello, there," she said cheerfully. "Is that Ana-Luisa, about whom I have heard so much?"

It was the lady from family court, I figured. She carried Ana-Luisa's stuffed animal that she had left in the driving school Dodge. I stood up and introduced myself and Ana-Luisa.

"Here's your toy, dear," the lady said, handing it to Ana-Luisa, who welcomed the stuffed animal's return. "Let's get acquainted, shall we? My name is Margaret Wood; I've been an officer of the family court for fifteen years." Ms. Wood, forty-ish, wore a black pantsuit and Nike running shoes. She carried a brown leather shoulder bag and a canvas satchel with the local public television logo, from which she pulled out a legal pad and pen.

"How are you, Ana-Luisa?"

Ana-Luisa looked to me.

"It's okay, sweetheart," I told her. "Tell Ms. Wood how you are."

Ana-Luisa put her head down. "My parents died," she said softly.

"I know, dear, and I am so terribly sorry," said Ms. Wood. "But my job is to make certain we find you a wonderful new home."

How awful, I thought: there are no new homes; there are only substitutes.

"I want Ana-Luisa to live with me," I said. "I feel we have a great deal in common, especially considering what we have been through today. I would like to raise her."

"Mr. Orr, please. I am aware of your good intentions, but, right now, I would like to speak to Ana-Luisa," said Ms. Wood.

"Ana-Luisa, to love, and be loved, is a child's right," she explained. "I am certain your parents loved you, but we live in a strange world, don't we?"

Ana-Luisa didn't answer.

Ms. Wood continued: "Alas, what you have experienced today is all too common. Families destroyed by modern life. Are you certain you have no other relatives?"

"I don't think so," Ana-Luisa said.

"Would you like to go to a new school?" Ms. Wood asked. "Would you like to live in a new neighborhood? You live on the Upper East Side, don't you, Mr. Orr?"

"I do," I answered.

"Would you mind, Ana-Luisa, if I spoke alone with Mr. Orr? An officer will keep you company," Ms. Wood said.

A policewoman appeared and held her hand out to Ana-Luisa. "Let's watch some TV down the hall, okay, hon?" she said.

"Not TV, not today," I said. "I don't think it's the best idea."

"Oh, yeah, okay. We'll go for a walk," the policewoman suggested.

"It's all right, Ana-Luisa. I'll be right here," I promised.

"It is very, shall we say, unusual for a single male to be accepted into the foster parents' program," Ms. Wood said when Ana-Luisa had gone off with the police officer. "But I understand this is an unusual case. According to our initial search on the computer, Ana-Luisa's mother was killed in a bodega shoot-out two years ago in their neighborhood. The mayor's office says crime rates have been declining in the past five years, but you can't prove it by me. Mr. Orr, if you wouldn't mind a few personal questions?"

"Please, Ms. Wood, ask me anything."

"I think it is very nice that you would want to provide a home for Ana-Luisa," she began. "But there are considerations. For instance: Do you consider yourself flexible? Do you have the energy to raise a child? Do you have any experience with children? Can you accept a child as he, or she, is without adding any unreasonable expectations? Could you cope if Ana-Luisa did poorly at school or demonstrated any behavorial problems in the new environment you will provide? Can you really afford to raise a child and send her through school? What happens if your newspaper folds, as is so often suspected, or if you are fired from your job at *View*? What would you do if, well, you became sick?"

"Those certainly are reasonable questions, Ms. Wood."

"There are more, Mr. Orr, many more," she continued. "Are you willing–do you understand the extent of the freedoms you will give up as a foster parent? Are you aware that you must, when you yourself are not available, provide sufficient child care and supervision? Are you willing to make your career secondary to Ana-Luisa and her needs?"

"I should find that a relief," I said.

"And what about providing Ana-Luisa with normal role models? Strong examples of people of the opposite sex? It's unlikely you will ever marry, isn't it?"

"Yes."

"Role models, Mr. Orr. Ana-Luisa will need positive examples of womanhood. She will need real parenting, not instant breakfasts."

"This is harder than getting a license to drive," I said, trying to make a joke.

"You're absolutely right, Mr. Orr," agreed Ms. Wood. "And passing tests does not seem to be your forte."

What could I say? "Ms. Wood, if I may? Your questions are thorough and valid. What can I say to convince you that I will try to do my absolute best to ensure that Ana-Luisa is raised with everything she will need to become a responsible, and successful, adult? All I can do is give you my word that I will. And tell you, again, that I know a little bit about what Ana-Luisa's life will be like. I know what happens when your parents die."

Ms. Wood yawned.

"I'll get letters from the governor; I'll get you letters of recommendation from the pillars of society!"

"The governor?"

"We're like this," I said, lying, and crossed my fingers.

"I'll be honest with you, Mr. Orr," she said and leaned forward. "I'm worried about all those society people you know."

"I'm worried about them, too," I said. "They've been a mess ever since the Reagans left the White House and the pouf skirt let them down!"

"That's not what I meant."

"Of course," I said and slumped back against the metal chair. "Don't think of me as one of them, Ms. Wood; think of me as a sportswriter, say, one who covers leagues and teams," I pleaded. "It is a job; despite the fancy suit, I am not my job."

"Armani, isn't it?" she asked.

"Yes," I answered.

"I wouldn't tell just anyone, Mr. Orr, but I'm not allergic to fashion. My sister is a pattern cutter for Donna Karan."

"Donna Karan, really?" I tried to sound as interested as possible; the truth was, my batted ribs ached.

"Donna's a piece of work; the stories my sister tells. You could get a week's worth of columns," Ms. Wood said, eyes bright.

"They're all pieces of work, Ms. Wood; we're all pieces of work! Anybody who lives long enough in New York City becomes 'a piece of work' just by breathing the air."

"You really want to keep Ana-Luisa, Mr. Orr?"

"I really do."

"But why? What is your real reason?" Ms. Wood asked. "Close your eyes, Mr. Orr, and look down the highway of life. Do you see yourself, five years from now, the father of a thirteen-year-old?"

In my youth, when I looked down this highway of life, I'd only seen Mick Jagger. I closed my eyes today and saw nothing. "Is loneliness the wrong answer?" I asked.

"Actually, yes, it is. Adopting a child, let alone having a child, in an effort to deny the loneliness of one's existence is a vain, egotistical reason for parenting. On the other hand, it seems that is what motivates the majority," Ms. Wood sighed.

She stood up; she extended her hand. "First things first, Mr. Orr. I will most likely recommend that Ana-Luisa be delivered into your custody; tonight she must stay in hospital for observation. It is customary after a day such as the one you both have had; I would suggest you seek some medical attention. You look awful."

"Thank you," I exclaimed, thinking only of Ana-Luisa and the chance we would soon become a family.

We found Ana-Luisa quietly sitting at the desk of the policewoman who kept her company during my interview with Ms. Wood. I explained to her what would happen next; I promised to visit her in the hospital before I went home to bed after work. I promised I would return tomorrow morning to take her to live with me. We hugged and said goodbye for now; I reminded Ms. Wood that she hadn't eaten yet today.

Ms. Wood gave Ana-Luisa her hand to hold. We decided not to leave the precinct at the same time because of the press outside. "Remember, Mr. Orr," Ms. Wood said before they walked away, "your custody of Ana-Luisa will be considered highly unorthodox; like all foster parents you will be assigned a case worker, who will visit frequently. A child, adoptive or natural, is a gift from God, Mr. Orr. In this case, it will be a gift from me."

A few minutes later I took a deep breath—not much bliss for my ribs—and braved meeting the press outside the police station.

"So, Julian, you got off! What really happened?" was one question called.

"Do you think you racially incited the driving teacher to violence?" was another.

"Is it true you made a pass at the driving teacher?"

"What about the little girl? You really want her to go to Brearley?"

"Ladies and gentlemen, friends and enemies," I began. "It has been a long day; you can read my version of what happened in tomorrow's *Tribune*." I thought my employers at the newspaper might like this extra-added promotion.

"Come on, Julian, no fair!"

"We've waited out here all afternoon!"

I walked toward Ninth Avenue to find a taxi.

"Fuck you, Julian!" a photographer yelled.

"Sorry, friend, I gave up sex three years ago."

Despite the acrid smell and sticky, rolling soda cans on the floor, it was a great relief, in this our little town of Bangladesh-with-Tinsel, to get inside the taxi and bomb down Ninth and across Broadway at Forty-fourth Street.

"What happened to you?" asked Ondine, the rather savvy German lady who ran the newspaper concession at the *View*. "I'm so sorry; I heard about the accident on the radio."

I bought a bottle of Spa water. The clock over Ondine's head read 5:30 P.M.

"You look bad; you should see a doctor."

"Think I'll freak everyone out upstairs?"

"They're fashion victims; tell them you were just photographed by Helmut Newton for an *Uomo Vogue* story on slam dancing," Ondine laughed. "Call your doctor," she repeated.

I promised I would.

My office, on the thirteenth floor of the building, was an ample box without a window to the street. Through a glass partition I looked into the antechamber of Ines Spring's minimalistically decorated office. Ines was in a meeting. My office was impossible to navigate because of a rack of clothes that had been rolled inside.

"Oh, no!" I cried, remembering the significance of the rack.

"Julian, is that you?" My assistant, Max, a peacefully sweet twenty-two-year-old, poked his head through the rack of clothes.

"Hi," I said.

"You look awful? What happened?"

"You haven't heard?"

"Did you get your license?"

"No."

"Not again," Max frowned.

"I see the skirts came," I said, pushing the rack of clothes to an angle so I could walk to my desk.

"Aren't they a riot?" Max asked.

These were not skirts for women; they were skirts for men. It appeared to be the rage that season for designers to include skirts for men in their fall collections; the fashion department at *View* thought an amusing article might be for me to wear a different skirt ensemble for a week in New York and keep a diary. The experiment was meant to commence tomorrow. Skirts for men? Ines had her doubts. "Every other year since World War II some designer thinks he'll get some extra press if he shows skirts for men; they never sell," she had said when the story idea was presented a few weeks before.

I vowed I would get myself out of having to do this story, especially now.

Among my messages was a call from the manager of the driving school; I rang him first thing.

"I trust you heard what happened?" I said.

"I can't believe it," he murmured.

"Were you very close to Hector?"

"I couldn't stand him; I'm upset about the car. It was one of our best Dodges."

Would it have been perverse of me to defend Hector's honor? To tell his manager that Hector was probably the most devoted employee he could have? That the Dodge was unbearable? Relax, relax, relax, I told myself.

"You there?" the manager asked.

"Yes, I'm here."

"The reason I called was because the boss, the owner of McCaulay's, isn't happy about the bad publicity he figures the school is going to get in the next few days, so he wants us to fix some kind of happy ending."

"Happy ending?"

"Yeah," the manager said. "We can get you the first road test tomorrow morning at Yonkers."

"Really?"

"Eight A.M. We leave from your place at 7:15; I'll drive."

"Let me think about it," I answered. "I'll call you back."

"Julian," a woman's voice came from beyond the rack of skirts. "Where have you been all day?" Maisie Dunne, one of the senior fashion editors on the magazine, emerged from the wools and silks and stood over me. "You're a sight. Have you been out slam dancing?"

British-born Maisie was a sight, too, certainly by so-called normal standards. Her blond wavy hair was put up every morning in a beehive; by the cocktail hour, Maisie's favorite time of the day, half of the hive had fallen. Tall and slender, she could have been the twin sister of Ichabod Crane. She wore a silver miniskirt, green tights, purple suede stiletto pumps, and a black T-shirt with "Take Me to Your Leader I Think I Love Him" sewn in sequins on its bodice. Every inch of limb was covered with baubles, bracelets, rings. Her eyes were lined with black kohl; her lips and nails were vamp red.

Maisie was a fashion institution. It was she who during an argument supposedly told Diana Vreeland to go to hell and "wash your child's hair in dead champagne" and this, with a different spin, became one of the late fashion editor's most famous lines.

"With all due respect, Maisie, because I know I agreed to do the story at first, I am not wearing those skirts around New York this week."

"What?"

"We'll have to drop the story, please."

"But I think you will look positively fierce in these," Maisie insisted and singled out a Black Watch kilt and gray wool henley sweater ensemble from the rack. "The idea is for the man who wears skirts to look rugged, like a girl who has just stepped off the lacrosse field."

"Can we discuss this with Ines, later?"

"You bet we will!" Maisie disappeared through the rack of skirts into the hall.

"Oh, Julian, your editor called from the newspaper to remind you to file as soon as you can," Max said.

I sat at my desk and considered the nature of the copy to be filed. I didn't want to do it. Nor did I want to go to Yonkers in the morning. I was tired; I wanted sleep. The significance of the day's happenings began to weigh on me.

The phone rang.

"Well, well." It was the shrink, Dr. Hooven. He had just heard the news reports on his car radio; he was calling from his Jaguar. I told him the whole story. I told him my plans for Ana-Luisa.

"When are you going to go for your road test?" he asked.

"I can go first thing in the morning, but I don't want to."

"What's the matter with you? After all the work we've done in therapy? Do you want your money back?" He paused. "Remember the snake, Julian."

"Oh, no, not the snake," I moaned. He referred to an incident that happened years ago at home in Goldenrod, something that later became a recurring dream until my dreams were taken over almost entirely by misbegotten nightmares of me driving, or not driving, as the case might have been.

One afternoon, the summer I turned thirteen, I heard my mother scream from the kitchen. I ran to her and saw on the floor before her a long, black snake that must have gotten itself inside the house through the open screen door from the garden. It slithered on the floor; my mother was in tears. I grabbed a broom; I tried to sweep the snake out, but it wouldn't budge. It coiled around the brushes; it slithered toward my mother. It was impossibly heavy to move. Finally, with as much strength as I could muster, I swept the snake outside and slammed the screen door closed.

My mother was inconsolable.

"Remember the snake?" the shrink repeated.

"I remember the snake."

"So you'll go tomorrow morning?"

"I'll go tomorrow morning."

The shrink's car entered the Lincoln Tunnel and ended our cellular connection; we hung up. There was a commotion in the hall outside Ines's office, a heated discourse among three of the fashion editors.

"The forties look is back," one of them said. "Divine!"

"I distrust nostalgia," a second opined.

"It's all about the new millennium," said another. "Designers are looking back in order to go forward."

"But the forties?"

"Our question is, do you think the forties and the Victorian period have anything in common in terms of design?" asked the third editor.

"Perfection! Sublime!" screeched the second lady. "Vivienne Westwood, forties-Victorian," she dreamed aloud. "That's our lead story: Silhouette! Bosom! Waist!"

I closed my office door and began to write the column; 900 words about learning to drive and what happens when your parents die. An hour later I filed the copy through the phone modem. Max went home; there was a knock on the door. Ines entered.

"How was jail?" she asked.

I told her everything. I told her about Ana-Luisa and my plan to become her foster parent; I begged not to have to wear the skirts.

"Life goes on, Julian," Ines said. "We only become more of who we already are. You can wait until Monday, but wear the skirts. Cash your paychecks; raise Ana-Luisa. Smile at perfume launches and, please, get yourself a personal life."

She was going home to see her children and to change her clothes. We arranged that she would come back to the office in an hour so we could go together in her car to the perfume launch that night at the Statue of Liberty.

Vanity, no stranger, reminded me I was not sporting a particularly pretty face that day. I went to the beauty department and knocked on the door of the editor in charge.

"It smells good in here," I said.

"It should; it's the beauty department," replied Dorothy Carson, the editor.

"I'm sorry to trouble you, Dorothy, but is there anything I can do with my face before I go to the perfume launch with Ines?"

Dorothy swung into action. My bruises were painted pale with creams and powders. I borrowed a Calvin Klein two-button blue suit off a rack of clothes intended for a Sean Penn shoot later in the week; I washed and changed in the men's room.

Back in my office, I called the driving school manager and told him we were on for the next morning. I called Ana-Luisa at the hospital to see how she was doing.

"I'm okay," she said.

"Have you eaten?"

"I had ice cream."

"You need to eat more; let me talk to the nurse."

"It's okay, Julian. I'll eat tomorrow."

"I miss you," I said.

"I know," Ana-Luisa whispered.

THIRTY-FOUR

...

When I was thirteen, my mother and Aunt Libby were Hanukah shopping in Hartford when my mother fell near a display of cashmere sweaters.

She was ill.

"My mother's going to die," I told Aunt Libby that evening when she drove alone to our house to tell me my mother was in the hospital.

"Don't be ridiculous, Jules," my aunt said.

"I'm thirteen now; you can tell me the truth."

Aunt Libby shook her head and wrapped herself in the Persian lamb coat my mother had given her for her last birthday.

It was snowing that evening; we drove without sound to the hospital in Goldenrod, where my mother was taken by ambulance after initial treatment by the doctors in Hartford. She was put in the Saul H. Orr Memorial Room; there was a bronze plaque on the door to commemorate a 1963 donation to the hospital from my father's estate.

My mother was asleep. Through the clear plate-glass window the snow danced in the lights from the town.

Aunt Libby stroked my mother's arm. "Leah, wake up, I've brought Jules."

My mother opened her eyes; frozen green ponds that registered only defeat. I smiled; she closed her eyes on tears and fell back asleep.

A hospital volunteer arrived with a small Christmas tree; there didn't seem any point in thwarting her enthusiasm. I sat on the edge of my mother's bed and waited for her to awaken. So I had grown, I realized; my feet touched the ground.

My mother turned on her side. "Jules," she murmured.

"Mom?"

"Have you eaten?"

"Yes," I lied.

She closed her eyes. I smoothed her auburn hair; I noticed for the first time that the roots were white. Aunt Libby walked toward the window and the snow.

In Goldenrod, there were often blizzards; until now they always kept outside.

THIRTY-FIVE

...

B̲een chatting up our sainted beauty director?" Ines asked as I got into the back seat of her chauffeur-driven Cadillac.

"How do I look?"

Ines did not respond. She rubbed her fingers with a wet Kleenex; her children, a boy and a girl, were decorating seashells with tempera paint when she got home, she explained. Some of the colors were still on her hands. "I don't expect you will be the only man wearing full makeup at the Statue of Liberty tonight," she laughed.

The car delivered us to the ferries that sailed to the Statue of Liberty; waiters served champagne in crystal flutes on silver trays. Ines wore a Chanel suit made of umpteen thousand gold sequins; they played well in paparazzi camera light. No less than two thousand people were there: society, fashion types, media personalities, actors making the scene to promote recently released films, and supermodels mixed with the other usual suspects. Towering above the festivities was Lady Liberty herself, the Mona Lisa of immigration.

It was a party to launch a perfume called Liberté, a new scent from the French designer Maldoror, a major fashion-society force certainly in the seventies and early eighties, still an important advertiser in *View*. Because the Parks Department had not allowed the organizers of the event to install special lighting at the statue, it was a rather dark affair except for several thousand votive candles.

"Who lighted the candles?" Ines joked as we walked toward a familiar face in the dark.

"I smell spring in the air," wheezed Nan Dancer, the famously thin socialite oft-noted for her Maldoror couture frocks, which the design house gave her for free. She air-kissed us hello.

"The Japanese press have been all over me tonight," she said to no one in particular. "It's so dark I keep squinting; they think I'm one of them," she laughed. We didn't. Nan Dancer wafted off toward Bill Blass and Oscar de la Renta.

We walked on a red carpet under a white canopy toward the bloated figure of the once handsome designer Maldoror. He held court, and a bottle of his Liberté, in an area separated from the rest by a red velvet rope and bodyguards. His partner, Andre Sabatier, a minister of culture in France, greeted Ines with kisses and flourishes. I took notes for my newspaper column of the people who were there.

"Darling, darling, darling," Andre Sabatier breathed into Ines's ear.

She congratulated him on the extravaganza; he noticed she was not wearing Maldoror.

"Extravaganza? Doing something like this is not an extravaganza. It's second nature for us; a picnic it is just," he sniffed.

In 1977, the House of Maldoror had launched one of its scents in New York by chartering a southern showboat; everyone said it was the party of the decade. Afterward, fortified by a surfeit of vodka and whatever else, Maldoror and his entourage retreated to Studio 54 and found oblivion by dawn.

"Ines, pet," Maldoror slurred, dropping his air kisses on Ines's shoulders, "come with us tonight when we go to Studio 54."

"Studio 54 closed several years ago, darling," Ines said.

Maldoror took this news as a personal slight, it seemed; he turned his back to Ines and groped for his boyfriend, an aging blond with a ponytail who was famous in France, in the seventies, for making several adult films.

"I guess we can leave now," Ines said.

"Why not?" I asked.

Red, white, and blue fireworks exploded over New York harbor; a band played Beethoven's Fifth. Fireworks spelled "Liberté" in the sky. The producer of a fashion news show asked to interview Ines; she obliged.

As I waited, a man with pink face and bulbous, bald head presented himself.

"Aren't you from Goldenrod, Connecticut?" he asked.

"I am."

"Do you have any pull there?"

"Excuse me?" I yelled over the sounds of the fireworks.

"My name is Frank Benkov. I'm the one who bought the Goldenrod Inn and redid it."

The Goldenrod Inn, once a great private estate, was, in my childhood, a flophouse that had been vacated for as long as I could remember. I had read of its recent renovation into a spa, a weekend getaway for the overweight and overpaid. It was also a popular place, because of its three-hour proximity to New York, for people to rehearse their muscles after face-lifts and assorted other plastic surgery procedures.

"Our press agent has been trying to get you to stay at the Inn," Mr. Benkov continued. "It would be a great angle if you wrote about going home by way of staying in our spa."

I smiled diplomatically; my bruises hurt.

Mr. Benkov was hard to appease. "What's wrong with you that you don't want a fabulous weekend for free?" he asked.

"Journalists aren't meant to accept free trips," I said.

"Okay, what's your real reason?"

"And I don't have the time."

"I'll call you tomorrow," he insisted.

"Mr. Benkov, really. I have a rather peculiar relationship to Goldenrod."

"It's the rose of New England; did you know that?"

"Yes, sir, I did know that."

"You'll come and write when we open the casino; that's what I wanted to talk to you about."

"Casino?" I inquired.

"Haven't you read about it? There's a mental asylum right outside of Goldenrod I think I can get the state of Connecticut to close down and sell me, but my problem is the local town fathers need convincing—that's why I thought of you—because the asylum is right next to a Jewish cemetery. The Jews of Goldenrod," Mr. Benkov smirked, "seem to be putting up a stink."

"The dead Jews?" I asked.

My sarcasm eluded the gentleman.

"But we'll push it through. It'll cost us a little extra, but we'll spread a few bucks in the right direction. So who do you know?"

Red rose fireworks burst in the night sky.

"The only people I know in Goldenrod, Mr. Benkov, are buried in that cemetery."

He didn't hear me. "Can you imagine?" he yelled. "Yankee Jews—who would have thunk it? Yankee Jews?"

I had never wanted to hit a man before; I restrained myself. "My parents, Mr. Benkov, and all my aunts and uncles, are buried there!"

I felt a hand on my sleeve; it was Ines. "Let's go, Julian," she said.

"Ah, Miss Spring," Mr. Benkov said. "We meet at last."

Ines shook his hand and dropped it; we walked along the red carpet back to the ferries. More fireworks fell; Ines put on her dark glasses. We boarded the ferry for Manhattan; waiters offered port and cordials. "I don't know why you're so willing with strangers, Julian," Ines said. "It always makes you unhappy."

A Caribbean band banged on drums as the ferry slipped toward the city. Most New York parties are not picnics; you are a hostage in a gilded frame watching other people's pretty pictures dissolve. "Maybe you should see a doctor," Ines said when she dropped me at the Mid-Manhattan Hospital so I could look in on Ana-Luisa.

"I didn't tell you, did I? I'm going for my road test at eight tomorrow morning."

"Remember, Julian," Ines smiled, "it's hands at ten-to-two."

At the hospital, the nurse at the desk on the children's ward hesitated when I asked to see Ana-Luisa. I pleaded my case; she let me look in but wouldn't leave us alone. Ana-Luisa slept in one of six beds; she was near the window. I stood by her bed; she opened her eyes. "Where am I?" she asked.

"In the hospital, but just until tomorrow," I promised.

"Julian?"

"Yes?"

"I ate; the food was awful," Ana-Luisa smiled.

"Okay, you two, time for bed," the nurse said and escorted me out.

THIRTY-SIX

· · ·

My mother's doctors found a tumor on her brain; they would operate the day before Christmas that year.

The afternoon before the operation, Aunt Libby and I visited my mother in her room. Aunt Libby placed around the small Christmas tree put there earlier by the hospital volunteer the Hanukah presents she and my mother had bought on their last shopping trip: a white silk blouse, several bottles of Estée Lauder's Youth-Dew bath oil, a pair of Landlubber bell-bottom jeans for me that I had fancied when I saw them worn by rock stars on TV. My mother slept; when she awakened at one point, she saw the presents and asked that they be removed. "Take them," she begged. "Take them." Her face, this rose, closed and tightened with rage.

My mother fell back to sleep. The door to her room, the Saul H. Orr Memorial Room, opened. A half dozen carolers, dressed in wool scarves and caps like characters in Dickens, sang "Silent Night." One of the carolers handed me a bag from the local pharmacy filled with candy canes and chocolate Christmas bells.

In 1967, brain surgeons, before the advent of lasers, proceeded like explorers on Arctic expeditions. Like Eskimos cutting through ice to fish, the doctors sawed my mother's scalp open; a nurse shaved her head bare. The operation took eight hours; on Christmas Day we waited for her to awaken in the intensive care unit. To be honest, I understand little about my mother's demise in the medical sense; I was too young for her doctors to talk to, and we certainly did not have death therapy, where we discussed "feelings."

The doctors said the tumor was benign; nonetheless, my mother died three years later, the last two years of her life confined to a hospital bed in a sanitarium on the outskirts of Goldenrod. My teenage years were spent in a variety of ways: imitating hippies and writing free verse, mostly I remember constantly wondering first if, and then when, my mother would die. Aunt Libby wasn't the one to ask, nor were my other aunts and uncles, who were now grandparents slipping into their own dotages or bodily breakdowns. My mother's doctor would not take my call; I called persistently for a week until, when his receptionist couldn't take it any longer, he came to the phone.

"Is my mother going to die?" I asked.

"It's hard to say." he answered.

"Is she?"

"Well, there are many factors to consider, young man, one of which is the fact that we are all going to die someday," the doctor equivocated.

"What does my mother have, and is she going to die?" I repeated.

"You're too young, son, to talk to," the doctor said and hung up.

After about ten days in the intensive care unit, my mother was moved back to the Saul H. Orr Memorial Room, and, for the next couple of weeks, her spirits were remarkably good. She quickly regained the majority of her motor faculties; she learned to walk again, and she spoke without impairment. Her head remained wrapped in a turban of surgical gauze until a wig for which she had been measured arrived custom made from a hair salon in New Haven.

From the Goldenrod Hospital my mother was taken, four weeks later, to a hospital in the central part of the state that specialized in radiation treatment. It was there that something must have gone wrong; it wasn't explained. Perhaps the radiation therapy caused scarring of the brain tissue; my mother came home six weeks later withdrawn and unnerved. Her hair grew back white and coarse; her auburn wig, too bouffant, its lining scratchy, annoyed her and she stopped wearing it. She no longer dressed; she wore housecoats and nightgowns. She spent her days either in bed in her lavender room or, on what was considered a good day, dozing in her favorite Queen Anne chair in the family room in front of the TV. For all to see were the scars on her scalp; these purplish lines of surgery as entrenched as the borders of my father's ancestral Russia.

My grades at school, meanwhile, began to fall, and a counselor called on my mother to suggest I go away to a boarding school; Enfield, a private academy for boys in northeastern Connecticut, was recommended. My cousin Sarah drove me to my interview that spring; the school, although formidable and traditional, seemed appealing enough. That autumn I was enrolled.

The morning I left for Enfield was the last time my mother and I would ever have a sustained conversation again. She sat in her chair waiting for me to say goodbye; a car and driver had been hired to drive me the hour's distance north to Enfield.

"I don't want to go," I said.

"It's probably a good idea that you do go, however," she responded. "Write me letters; tell me how you find your new world. You are my eyes now."

I sat on the ottoman before her; she held my hands. "They don't know anything about the brain; I shouldn't have let the doctors touch me," she began.

"You'll get better," I insisted.

"You have to believe that, don't you, Jules? You're still a child."

I was silent.

"We've become a family of swans, haven't we? Sailing serenely on the water's surface, and no one sees how fast our feet move underneath in fear."

I heard the driver knock at the front door; he began taking my suitcases to the car.

"The evening before my operation I got out of bed and wrapped myself in one of those hideous hospital blankets. It was snowing outside; I watched the snow fall," my mother told me. She wouldn't let go of my hands. "I remembered that no two snowflakes are meant to be the same. I looked for the difference, but I couldn't find it; all I saw was white, one blinding white. Everything was the same; I thought I would try to remember some things, different things: When did my father die? When did my mother die? When did your father die? What day were you born? I couldn't remember. All I knew was it was snowing. A tumor on the brain? How could that be? Was it contagious? Would it happen to you? I remembered my mother; she came to me like a dream and brushed my hair."

The door to the Saul H. Orr Memorial Room opened; two nurses had come to prepare my mother for surgery the next morning. She was instructed to remove her hospital gown; she remembered she was asked to sit in the chair near the window, where she was covered with towels. Another nurse arrived with a tray and some instruments. Somehow, no one had sufficiently prepared my mother for the obvious: her head would have to be shaved before surgery. The nurse who was to do the barbering had a German accent, my mother recalled; this only added to her fear. My mother screamed, she said, in Yiddish, and tried to flee; she knocked over vases of flowers from friends and relations. The nurses subdued her; they strapped her into the chair and covered her mouth with a bandage.

Christmas carolers opened the door; a nurse locked it behind them. They shaved her head. The razor nicked her; she bled. The hair was removed in a brown grocery bag. One of the nurses held a mirror before my mother. "It isn't so bad," she said and sedated my mother with an injection.

Before she awakened after surgery, my mother said, she had dreamed of her mother. "I expected she would be there; of course, she wasn't," my mother remembered. "I wished she were there."

Aunt Libby knocked on the door of the family room; it was time for my leave.

I wish I had stayed.

For a while, that first year at Enfield, Aunt Libby, at my mother's insistence, would drive her to the school, but they would never stop. My mother, Aunt Libby explained, did not want to be a bother to me. I would be alerted by my advisor, who would have received a call from Aunt Libby, that they would be driving by that afternoon. I would sit on the stone wall outside the chapel at Enfield and wait for the Pontiac to go past.

They never stopped.

Aunt Libby drove; my mother waned in the passenger's seat.

The fall of my junior year at Enfield my advisor took me aside after chapel one Sunday morning and told me he had received a call from Goldenrod. It was "time," he said. I went home in a hired car with a driver that afternoon, and Aunt Libby and I drove to the sanitarium where my mother was dying. We sat by her bedside until late that night; my mother, unconscious, struggled for breath.

"How long before she dies?" I asked the nurse.

"Quiet," she responded. "She can hear you; the hearing is the last thing to go."

An hour later, the nurse suggested I go home. "You've seen enough," the nurse said. "She is already bleeding internally. It may become external."

I walked outside, down the hall to where Aunt Libby drank coffee in a waiting room. I sat down; we didn't speak. Later, the nurse came for us. "It's over," she said.

"While we were out of the room?!" I said.

"It's over," the nurse repeated.

We returned to the hospital room; all was quiet now. My mother, at death, was diminished to the weight of a young girl. The scars of her scalp where her hair had never grown back were blue; she was covered in white.

But she died while I was out of the room. I am good with dead people now. I was there when Aunt Libby died a few years later, for instance.

You close your eyes and smooth the dyings' brows and imagine their spirits rippling into heaven. Help plan the funeral. Let the dying confuse you with others; we'll all be together in the great by-and-by. And discourage bedside truth tellings; the truth, like memory, is just another opinion.

THIRTY-SEVEN

...

The newapapers were at my doorstep at 6 A.M.

I got out of bed, sore ribs and swollen face, and looked for the reports of the accident with Hector and Ana-Luisa the day before.

Luckily, I think, it was not front-page news in the tabloids after all. The *Post*, the *News,* and the *Tribune* went with the more universally appealing story, I suppose, of Elizabeth Taylor's latest divorce. Our story was covered, of course, and the nature of the reporting depended on the politics and tone of the newspaper. The tabloids pretty much played up the idea of Hector as a man gone berserk; the *Times* suggested he was undone by the oppressiveness of racial issues that were manifested by the dynamic between us in the car.

The potentially inciteful fact that Hector was shot by the police was dealt with by craftfully collaborated statements of the investigating lieutenant and Eddie Bankhead. Hector had fired first, they readily assured reporters. Meanwhile, and quite rightly, the grandchildren of the black woman hit and killed during our driven rampage through Queens said no matter what happened, or who was to blame, their loved one wasn't coming back.

As for my reportorial contribution, the column was not jumped to the front page of the *Tribune;* in fact, it appeared next to the weather map on page twenty-six, some twelve pages back from where the column normally ran. Clearly, my days were numbered at the *Tribune.* It was inevitable on both parts; it was time to move on.

Speaking of motion, I got my license without dramatic detail that morning. It took all of twenty minutes driving without bold mistakes around Yonkers with an examiner. I was back in the city by 10 A.M. and headed straight to the hospital, where I hoped Ana-Luisa would be released in my care.

In the hospital lobby I happened to run into my M.D., Dr. Stanley Firbank, ever the colorful one. He wore a red turtleneck and was deeply tanned. "Girlfriend," he called when he saw me, "don't you think you need a doctor?"

"For marrying or for medical supervision?" I asked.

"Sorry, honey, but you're not my type."

Dr. Firbank, who read about my incident in the newspapers, examined me in a nurse's office. He prescribed an ointment for my bruises and painkillers but found nothing seriously wrong. "Rough trade, huh?" he joked as he felt my ribs.

"Just rough," I answered.

Upstairs I found Ms. Wood chatting at the nurses' station.

"There's an aunt," she said by way of greeting me. "She's inside with Ana-Luisa now."

I was dejected. "You mean?"

"Sorry, Mr. Orr. If you want to have a child, you'll have to try the old-fashioned way," Ms. Wood laughed.

"I can see Ana-Luisa, can't I?"

I followed Ms. Wood into the hospital room. Ana-Luisa was dressed in new clothes: blue denim overalls and a red-and-white-striped shirt. A woman, fiftyish and motherly, was showing her photographs of members of their family. They spoke Spanish and laughed. Ana-Luisa looked up and for just a moment seemed sad.

"I am Ana-Luisa's aunt Consuelo, and you have been very kind," the woman said, giving me her hand to shake.

"Oh, well, sure," I responded.

Aunt Consuelo and Hector were brother and sister, she explained; they had fought over money several years ago and not seen each other since. Her eyes flooded with tears when she mentioned his name; she held Ana-Luisa to her bosom. "Now I can make it up to Hector; we never should have fought. Ana-Luisa will be very happy in Trenton; her cousins cannot wait for her to come home."

It was time to leave. "You take care of your aunt, Ana-Luisa," I said.

She smiled. We said goodbye.

I took a taxi to my office; most everyone was already at lunch when I got there.

I didn't know what to do with myself, except work. I closed my door and wrote an uninspired column about the perfume launch; 900 words, of which the majority was a list of names of those who had attended the party. "The guests included" began the long list. After nearly eight years of writing an around-the-town column, I supposed "the guests included" could be my epitaph.

But I wasn't dead yet; in fact, I filed the column a good thirty minutes before deadline. The afternoon presented itself as a barren field without Ana-Luisa. The expectations of what I, as a new parent, might need to do were for naught; now I was to begin new again. I stared at the rack of men's skirts; I wasn't keen to wear one just yet, although the reportorial experiment might provide therapeutic distraction. I could return phone calls from several dozen publicists, but that meant giving countenance to another series of perfume launches and the like.

Then it occurred to me: I had my license; why not rent a car and go for a drive? Only by my denying it had Goldenrod assumed a distance in my mind of several thousand miles. In my emotions it was never far away; in reality, with improved highways, I could be there in less than three hours.

I was going home.

THIRTY-EIGHT

· · ·

A trip to Goldenrod, nearly a year after my mother died:

Aunt Libby, to whom my mother had left our house as a thank you for taking care of her during her illness, had sold the place at a loss. It was my first year at college; I already was scrambling for dollars to pay for tuition. My mother's estate, except for the value of the house, was almost nothing. Aunt Libby had promised to help me out financially as soon as she could; she wanted me to come home and help her pack.

I took a taxi from the train station; coming up the driveway I saw that the "For Sale" sign now said "Sold." Aunt Libby met me at the door; as was the case since my mother first became ill, we were mostly silent in each other's company. That afternoon I filled nearly thirty plastic garbage bags with the stuff of our lifetime; there were many things to be discarded — better items were marked for charity thrift shops. Aunt Libby said she could not bear to pack away my mother's clothing; I would.

We took a break and went for a walk on the lawn. The afternoon was autumn cool; the leaves were changing colors. We stopped at my father's sundial. "Come along with me, the best is yet to be," read the inscription.

Aunt Libby wore a brown tweed skirt and a wool cardigan sweater. She shivered, despite the sun.

"Do you ever see ghosts?" I asked.

"Sometimes," she answered.

"I do, too."

"But they are only memories, Julian, entertained as a way to assuage loneliness," Aunt Libby said. "You'll be fine; you're young. You'll get through college and probably will become a writer if you work very hard at it. And someday you'll marry and start your own family. Life goes on."

I wondered.

"I went to New York last weekend. I saw my mother and father."

"Julian, don't." Aunt Libby walked alongside the brook, over the bridge, and stood underneath the pagoda my mother had built.

"I did," I continued. "In the Astor Place subway. I saw two men; one was my father. I recognized him. I ran after him through the station, this man, my father. I ran so fast my eyeglasses fell off. Then the subway came. There was all this steam and fog, and I lost my father there. He was gone again."

"Dear," Aunt Libby sighed.

"Then, Aunt Libby, I saw a woman wearing this blue silk dress spotted with golden thread. She wore a tremendous hat with feathers, long black gloves, and she held on a leash two terriers, one black and the other white. A porter followed her; he carried my mother's suitcases. The woman, I recognized, was my mother. Your sister," I said.

"Please, Julian, dear." Aunt Libby began walking back toward our house.

I followed her. "She carried a bouquet of white iceberg roses, just like the ones that won my father the Rose of New England prize two summers before he died."

Aunt Libby raised her hand to silence me; she went inside and continued packing.

I did the same in my mother's room, the lavender boudoir. I began to pack her things; I opened the mirror-lined doors of her dressing-room closets segregated for the seasons, summer, winter, spring, and fall. I began folding blouses; the chill of silk burned my hands. Made in France, Made in Italy, Made in England, but to be worn where?

Did my mother love me?

I was cold; what could the matter be? I took off my flannel shirt and wrapped myself in a black cashmere cardigan with a full mink collar. I sat on the edge of my mother's bed; I removed my socks and shoes and my blue jeans. I pulled on a pair of black silk stockings. Then, around my neck, I fastened a strand of pearls and, on my feet, beige and black shoes.

"Look at me, look at me; I look like Mommy."

I wore a black, pleated cashmere skirt made by Marc Bohan for Christian Dior. I wore a Cartier tank watch on my wrist, an aquamarine ring with diamonds on my finger. My hair was brown, my forehead high; my eyes looked like Mommy's.

"Go to the top drawer." Her voice.

Inside was her black widow's veil; I put it over my head and heard inside the sounds of the sea against the sand that is always dancing. The veil was heavy and wet; my father now helped me carry it. He called me; I came closer. He took my hands and held them in the lap of my mother's skirt.

"When you die," he said, "you go deep into a blue sea. There is a hiss, Julian, a hiss of sound and color all yellow and bright. There is a song of would-be sorrow; you move yourself. Your arms follow; you swim or fly, it is all the same now. Some creature then, something like a tortoise, comes to you. He is armed with swords, these blades of crystal and silver; you follow. You'll know his face; it is clenched tight as an old man's fist. You put your hands, he tells you to, upon his chest and off you go, and go, and go but at a tortoise pace. There is no tick, no tock, no noise, no crash, no place too quick or sharp to fear.

"After death, Julian, there is no place to come or go; you are anyplace."

My mother watched as my father spoke; she listened. She glided toward the dressing-room mirrors; she brushed her auburn hair with a silver comb. My father came up behind her; his hands rested on her shoulders. He wore a black mask now; "The best is yet to be," he promised. She rested her head in his hands; he put a finger to his mouth lest I speak.

Still, I screamed: "ABCDEFGHIJKLMNOPQRSTUVWXYandZ!"

"Sssh, Julian," he said. "Follow me."

We left the house and walked across the lawn, under a lavender sky, into the woods. Something cool slid across my feet; it rippled into the brook. Leaves fell; zebra finches dipped for seeds. I followed my father into the brook; there was no fear, no tick, no tock . . . no noise, no rush, no place too quick or sharp. No place to go, no place to stay. From underneath the water I saw my parents by the sundial.

That was a dream, I trust; I awakened on my mother's bed wearing her clothes.

I packed; the house was sold. My last trip to Goldenrod was two years later, in summer, when Aunt Libby died.

THIRTY-NINE

· · ·

Yes, I learned to drive, but, frankly, I wouldn't recommend myself as an ace motorist; I don't think I'm very good.

My mind is all over the road, and I suspect my vision, although corrected by top-of-the-line contact lenses, isn't all that reliable, especially in the dark.

It was a clear, sunny, blue-skies, no-clouds sort of day when I ventured toward Goldenrod. I picked a lane, any lane, and headed up Third Avenue to the FDR Drive. I braked for errant cars, mostly New Jersey licensed – I can report it is true what they say about Garden State drivers – and followed the signs for New England.

My hands never wavered from a position of ten-to-two.

I veered left, veered right. Paid the tolls. Zoomed through Westchester, Stamford, Greenwich, and took the high road around New Haven. I stopped for coffee at Branford; back in the rented Ford I played the radio low lest popular love songs distract me.

The turnpike forked near New London; I kept to the left for Goldenrod. There were three exits to the town; I remembered to take the first and, soon enough, found myself driving along the streets of my childhood. It is true what they say about hometowns; they grow smaller the longer one keeps away.

Here was Main Street; I turned onto Terry Avenue and drove behind our house, the house we lived in when my father was alive. There were no cars in the driveway and not a sign of any roses left on the back lawn. Someone had painted the house mustard yellow, and it had gone to seed. I parked the rented car and walked on the lawn of our house; no one saw me, no one called out. I suppose the neighbors, if any of them were left the same, were all at work still; Michael's house next door was for sale.

Down a bit on Terry Avenue a woman sat in a rocker on the porch of what was once Mrs. Stanley's house. I walked nearer; the woman rocked in her chair; she smiled. I stopped.

"Hello," I called.

She nodded.

"I grew up on this street," I explained.

"In which house?" she asked.

"In the house that is now painted yellow."

"What's your name?" she asked.

"Julian Orr."

"No, it isn't," she said.

"It is, really."

This woman, heavyset with gray hair, studied me. "You asshole, Julian, you never came back." She got up from her chair and went inside.

I walked to her porch and looked inside the screen door. The house, which I remembered once busy with color and Mrs. Stanley's mendings, was a wreck of dull browns. The woman reappeared holding a picture in a frame; she opened the door. "Do you remember when this was taken?"

Dana Deamour showed me a gray photograph of us together.

"That was the summer my father died," I remembered. "Our mothers had taken us to the beach."

"That's right. Where've you been?"

Somewhat nervously, I told Dana Deamour about my life in the city. "I haven't been to Goldenrod in almost twenty years," I said. "Everyone has died."

"Not everyone," she said.

"Yes, of course not," I smiled.

"My mother's still upstairs, sick as a dog, sleeping most of the time. I'd take you up, but what's the point? Me, I live here, on money from the state. Remember Mrs. Warner? She's still around. She's found God; she only drinks on weekends now. I call on her, see how she's doing," Dana said. "Otherwise, the only news around here is that they want to build a casino outside of town. How about that?"

"I've heard," I said. "It's near where my parents, and most of my relations, are buried. That's why I've come today, to pay my respects."

"Well, I'm all for it. Life's a gamble, might as well build a casino."

I had many questions, but I did not feel it was my place to ask them, except one. "What became of my friend, Michael, who lived next door to us?"

"He lives on Mars," she answered. "Have a look." Dana pointed to the sky through maple trees.

"I should probably get going," I said, "if I want to get to the cemetery before dark."

"Suit yourself." Dana Deamour rocked in her chair. "Hey, Julian," Dana called after me as I walked toward the car. "If you're really a writer, why don't you write?"

Through the town, past the old Pontiac garage and the other shops vacated when the malls were built on the outskirts of town, I drove.

The road curved; there was a bridge and then no houses or buildings for a while until I saw the cluster of elm trees at the state hospital. I parked the car by the gate of the cemetery and looked on the ground for the perfect stones to place on my parents' graves.

I opened the gate to the cemetery and walked north, regarding the other graves with respect. This is my family now, I thought, our home. Toward the old stone fence, past the alley of birch and amber trees not yet enjoying the full bloom of spring, I found my parents' graves and those of my other relations. I balanced the stones as Jewish tradition decreed, so my parents would know I was there.

"It's me; I'm here," I whispered.

The stone on my mother's grave fell; I replaced it. My hands, caught in the late afternoon sunlight, were like puppet shadows on her gravestone. Was the ground keeping green enough here?

"It's me; I'm here," I repeated.

I cried.

What happens when your parents die? You become who you are without them; the same, but always their child, without them. It has become fashionable, it has been for some time, to question one's parents, to sometimes hate them when the reasons are good enough. But they are your highway. Fight the tolls; forgive the roads. Cry in the right place now.

You come back to yourself, your hands ten-to-two, despite the wheeling vagaries of memory.

What else?

Just that, of course, I wish they were here.